ROCK[illegible]E

and other short stories

ROCKS IN A LANDSCAPE

and other short stories

David Stuart

Matador
5 Weir Road
Kibworth Beauchamp
Leicester LE8 0LQ, UK
Tel: (+44) 116 279 2299
Fax: (+44) 116 279 2277
Email: books@troubador.co.uk
Web: www.troubador.co.uk/matador

ISBN 978 1848769 205

British Library Cataloguing in Publication Data.
A catalogue record for this book is available from the British Library.

Typeset in 11pt Garamond by Troubador Publishing Ltd, Leicester, UK

Matador is an imprint of Troubador Publishing Ltd

Dedicated to Family and Friends

Several stories chosen from those written over the past Twenty five years

CONTENTS

SUNRISE ON THE A180

As he begins to turn onto the slip road that leads down to the A180 he knows that something is wrong. The engine splutters and then cuts out. He draws the vehicle onto the hard shoulder. The fuel gauge…it just can't be relied on. Taps it, but it stays stubbornly on quarter full. Been caught out before, but not at 6 a.m. three minutes into his journey to Liverpool. Another bad day?

It's not a good place to stop either and it won't be long before the police are along. He speaks to John on his mobile. The 5 gallon can. In five minutes. No problem. All he has to do is wait.

He gets out of the vehicle, walks round it to see that it's as well parked as it can be in the circumstances, and then clambers up the two metres of grassy bank which gives him a view along the A180, and across to the Humber bank itself.

At first he can hardly make sense of what he sees. Behind industrial installations a mile or so away, the sun is just rising, its rays compressed fiercely by a wedge of cloud above it & partly barred by the structures in front of it. But it is the white confusion in the foreground which he can hardly focus on. Shading his eyes, he sees that the fields and waste land between the road and the bank are covered in a quilted eiderdown of white mist tinted with gold by the sun. Orange tongues of sun slide between the uprights of tubing and pipework, distorting the storage tanks, chimney stacks and buildings as if by their searing heat. Here and there patches of mist are dispersing, and a hedgerow here, a clump of trees there, and a derelict farm building are surfacing. He watches entranced, for sixty seconds or so. Then turns to look back along the road to Grimsby.

Here the sun is only just touching the taller buildings…the Telephone Exchange, a cluster of dockyard cranes, the Dock tower, the tower blocks beyond Freeman Street, Hewitts building, the ornate clock tower on that Education office building behind the old market, and even the tower and flag mast of St. James' Church. Then as he watches, the sun's rays break through onto the roofs of houses in West Marsh, coaxing their inhabitants into shaking off sleep, and getting on with a new day.

He pictures his wife, turning over in bed, loathe to escape its comfort, yet disturbed by the wakening light on the curtains. Soon she will be getting up, rousing the children, preparing their breakfast, getting them off to school, before she gets off to work herself. The same magic will be teasing the houses and parks and shopping malls across the whole town from Waltham to Wybers Wood, though how many it will transform is another matter. While he… assuming John is along pretty soon with that fuel… will be away, spinning along the familiar route: A180, M180, M18 , M62 and Liverpool.

The way the sun touches on the town, and now on fields and road itself, dispersing the mist like a flame-thrower, fills him with a sort of satisfaction. The ordinariness of life, its dullness, the routines, are not absolute. Each morning those same routines are infinitesimally modified and made unique by the newness of the day. Even if, unlike today, it is one of those dull murky starts. No day is a replica of the last one, or the next one.

There was the row with his wife last week, words he regretted; once again it was all about the older girl staying out at night, her attitude to school. On top of that the awkward hours the firm expected him to work, her modest wages, and the pokey house they were obliged to live in. When were they able to enjoy a decent night out together? But none of these things were final or irrevocable. What was that annoying word their daughter's school report had used: 'outcomes' …well, anyhow, those outcomes can always change, can get better, or even get worse. Things move on. Potentials are revealed, opportunities arise, and can be taken up or just wither away. That sun sees to that. It is a kind of celestial guarantee of a daily fresh start. And it comes every twenty-four hours.

He looks back at the vehicle and grins wryly. A police car is just drawing up, and a policeman and policewoman in orange and green glow jackets get out. He slithers down the bank. 'Run out of fuel,' he says to them. 'My mate will be here any minute.' She nods, casting a critical eye at the back of his vehicle as they always do. The other one is round the front. And just as he turns to rejoin them the sun cuts across the flyover onto the slip-road. The two of them and their gaudy police car, explode into flames. 'Okay,' she says,' and then smiles. 'As long as you get it moved as soon as possible.' It is too early, and too beautiful a morning, for officiousness or malice.

Out of the corner of his eye, he sees John's van approaching the fly-over.

It is strange how an everyday object lurking in some forgotten corner, can surface unexpectedly and haunt us. The resurrected image, like some single piece of a jigsaw found under the sofa, demands we find a place for it, resolve its problem status. One such object sits in my garage, and has done so for as long as I can remember. Then the other day I spilled some green paint, the colour of tinned peas, and its anonymity was suddenly shattered. It was my mother's wooden tea trolley. The colour of the peas was an especial reminder.

It's old and shabby though reasonably robust. We don't use it as trolley, I don't know whether we ever have, but it's usually jammed up against the back wall of the garage, loaded with tins of paint, bottles of turps, and oddments.

'Look, why don't we throw that thing out?' my wife suggests. 'There's a jumble sale at the Chapel next week.'

'Oh, you never know,' I usually say, 'we might need it.'

And yet at the same time I know I dislike the thing; an ugly and uncertain image of drudgery hangs over it. I know it ought to go. My mother would have been the last person to suggest that we hang onto it. But it is as if there is, for me, some unsettled business attached to that trolley.

We were living in a flat, the top floor of a city centre office block, actually called 'Chambers' where my Father under normal circumstances was the caretaker. It was wartime and so while he was away working as a fireman on an East Coast oil jetty, the work of caretaking devolved on my mother. I think she hated it …the role I mean, but could not afford for the sake of the flat and three children, to be choosey. She had been an accounts clerk with the Savings section of the Central Post Office and had risen to a position of some responsibility before we had come along.

My mother's real passion was elocution and theatre. She learned great reams of Ophelia and Rosalind and even Hedda Gabler, declaiming them to, our acute embarrassment, in our front room on a Sunday evening, or even Sitwell-like from the windows of the flat which overlooked a busy shopping street in the city. Thank goodness she didn't go so far as to employ a megaphone; the words were only heard by the pigeons and sparrows. In later years she would throw herself into producing plays for amateur adult and youth drama groups. She attended University extension lectures on the modern theatre, and there were books on Stanislavski and Ibsen and Greek Tragedy on the shelves. However I don't think she would have held much store by anything as dull as 'Method' acting. She preferred the role of dynamic actor-director, whirling round the stage, conjuring dramatic movements from the actors, orchestrating their gestures and great speeches. The hidden meaning of the words that were delivered, and the way gesture could be used to enrich it, was so important to her. Even after the rehearsals, all hell would be let loose on the kitchen table and at the sewing machine as curtains were transformed into costumes, cardboard boxes into props. Actor-director-stage designer.

She loved to organise people, especially in dramatic situations. In fact, she exercised this talent on our everyday lives as children, and even on my Father when he came home on leave. A visit to the dentist, a day-out walking in the countryside with a spot of black-berrying thrown in, or a shopping trip to buy shoes, all were dramatic situations and encounters, with all their exits and entrances, nervous climaxes, and final curtains. It had the virtue of making life in the 1940s less dull and predictable which I suppose was an achievement for those dreary days. But at the time we three children didn't appreciate that.

The 'Chambers' where we lived however was quite another kind of stage and one on which my mother was uncomfortable. The role of producer here was not one she could relish. All the potential for dramatic tension was diffused by early hours, dust, buckets of coal, mops and carbolic fumes. She had responsibility for a huge bunch of keys and had to organise a team of cleaners who arrived each morning at 6 am. The offices of the solicitors, fire-assessors, architects and accountants had to be ready for 8.30 am. An old man came in to help with loading of buckets of coal and firewood from the basement. An ancient lift with heavy brass controls was used to bring them up to each of the four floors. There were ash buckets to be emptied, wastepaper to be collected. The man was a world-war one veteran with a gammy leg. Sometimes when the weather was bad, he didn't turn up and so my mother with the grudging assistance of my other brother and sister set about the job of loading and carting the buckets.

But it wasn't the hard physical work which my mother hated in all this, nor especially the early hours coupled with the additional task of getting us off to school. Nor did she deny the right of solicitors and such like to be fussy about their office comforts. No, my mother's hatred for the whole undertaking arose, I can see now, from its complete lack of poetic style or resonance. It was a kind of kitchen sink drama, but fifteen or twenty years before the genre's potential had been discovered.

The climax of all this drudgery was however an event that did have a kind of festive celebratory quality. Good Friday was

Spring Cleaning Day. The whole building was closed while every wall, staircase, corridor, door, skirting board, lamp fitting, fire surround, toilet fitment, concrete floor, stuccoed ceiling, and any uncovered item of furniture, was appropriately cleansed, scrubbed, or polished by an army of cleaning women. The usual six cleaners were augmented by friends and neighbours, thankful for the extra bob or two for Easter. The work took all day. The stairwell, the corridors, and even our flat on the top floor stank of ammonia and disinfectant, and echoed with the women's plaintive songs.

At midday the army had to be fed. Tradition had it ....the property owners had Quaker credentials I believe...that they should be given a proper meal. My mother prepared, cooked and served it. It was exciting for us to see the food for as many as twenty cleaners being prepared. A huge joint, especially allocated by the Food Ministry I suppose....the potatoes and vegetables (it was always peas!) in various saucepans, the battery of apple pies on plates. Woe betide if you got in the way. My mother didn't mind the chore of baking for this small army. She was at least mistress of that part of the undertaking. We were only allowed to help with moving stuff around & serving. But as Good Friday morning progressed she became increasingly agitated and then angry, noisy with the pans and plates. The climax of it all, the opening of the curtain so to speak, was direction of the extended moment when the food was served. And this was what she found most depressing and shaming, most devoid of poetry or opportunity for dramatic presentation..

Half a dozen trestle tables were set up in a foyer at the foot of a grandish staircase and here the army of cleaning women assembled. They were in their oldest clothes with tight scarves over their heads, voices loud and coarse, most of them smoking (who could blame them in that carbolic atmosphere, but my Mother was never able to tolerate smoking, whatever the person's class or gender!). And all of them or so it seemed to me looked pityingly on as my Mother and we three pushed the trolley out of the lift, that same wooden trolley, piled high with plates on which slivers of meat, mashed potatoes, and tinned peas shivered. The thin gravy was in a large jug and there was hardly enough for all. There were several journeys to be made. And then the pudding, always the same flat apple pie, segmented, with big jugs of a thin custard with a sturdy skin. The painstaking crawl of the lift and the long cold-scrubbed corridors before our triumphant entry must have given everything time to chill thoroughly. Especially the mashed potato, the gravy and the custard. Finally there were the cups of tea, which the women would have preferred with their pudding, but my mother would not entertain that. Even if it had been possible in terms of organisation, she would have vetoed it on grounds of etiquette.

Of course the women were polite. 'Thank you Mrs for a right good dinner,' someone would say, and 'lot of hard work for you and the kiddies,' someone else added. But apart from a half-hearted round of nods, I never felt this was any more than mere formality. They could see that she hated the whole thing. At the most dramatic moment, the passing round of the plates, and the first dig and scoop with the array of utensils we had managed to muster, she would turn away from their silence, shamefaced, it seemed to me. Of course, my present eye can see the pathos of it …but at the time I just found it inexplicably hollow and depressing, as it undoubtedly was for her. And then as we retreated to the lift, chatter would resume which soon became ribald, although we could never quite make out what was being said in that echoing foyer as we rode up to our top floor sanctum and our even more economical lunch.

So that trolley stands there as a reminder of a ritual drama which in a sense was a flop. Its producer was my Mother. And I am sure those women's cool assessment of my Mother was that she was miscast. That they thought her 'snobby' I don't doubt. There were some, the quieter ones, who would have liked to have shown some real warmth and friendliness, to her and her children. One did come and baby-sit on a Drama Group night. I was terrified that it might be Sadie Durance (The name is engraved on my memory …the deep and grating fifty-a-day voice echoing like some asthmatic sea-lioness let loose in the corridors of the Chambers). Fortunately, the baby sitter was one of the quieter ones. It was nice to see her dressed for going out rather than for scrubbing floors. And my Mother could chat with her in a friendly way, without seeming to be condescending.

But during the Good Friday production itself, my Mother set her face against any kind of intercourse or accommodation. She didn't want to be any part of it, not in any version. I can sympathise with her now.

In theory it might have been easy to be enthusiastic about equality and classnessness, the virtues of all pulling together on the scrubbed floors of second world war Britain. But in reality my Mother knew she had a lot to fight for, and a lot to cling onto. The Chambers were a place where her dramatic gifts and vocation would bear no fruit. She did her best in the circumstances, then she exited left, liftwards and upwards, drawing her offspring behind her. The shabby trolley will always remind me of that, and her Good Friday sacrifice.

WINDOWS

If you want to study philosophy probably one of the best places to do would be on the North face of the Eiger. The cold, the danger and the height would give your brain cells something to work on. So George and I, swinging gently in our respective cradles high up on the glass wall of an office block, have a fairly good everyday substitute. The building we're working on is called Pearsons Holdings; if you ask me what it's holding I couldn't possibly give you an answer. And we are a team; six of us today …cleaning the glass. Straightforward job as long as you have the right equipment and a head for heights. Can be boring but at least we're out in the open air. And the money is reasonable. Trouble is, me and George. We have to complicate things. Observing too much, doing too much thinking. Each in our own way.

Take this morning.. We were having our mid-morning break, the six of us, on the ground.

'You know,' I say, 'Up there, I was thinking. Two worlds.'

The others groan and one of them says, 'Not again.' George snorts. 'What you should be watching for is the talent. Have you seen that one on the fourth floor? I don't know how she dares to wear that skirt.'

The others want to know which window George is talking about. The trouble is, I know George a lot better than they do. We've been mates for a long time and I know he's as bad as me at letting his imagination run riot. I try to go along with the things he says, but I know the girl he's on about is either non-existent or just a vaguely feminine shadow deep inside the blue haze of the windows. She could be fifteen or fifty; Gwyneth

Paltrow or Old Mother Hubbard.

'Poor old George,' someone says eventually. 'Seeing things again.'

George stands up and wanders off, looking up at the building and the huge acreage of glass. I take my snap box back to the van, and then catch up with him.

'Take no notice,' I say. 'They're only jealous…'

'Maybe, 'he says. 'I know what I did see. Anyhow, what was that you was saying, About Two Worlds. Where?'

'That one inside that you see, blue-tinted, secretive, and me with the other one, outside, reflecting all the glory of the clouds and sky.'

'Oh yes,' says George, in supportive but puzzled sort of way. He is my mate.

So I try to explain again. With George it isn't so much explanation he needs, more a kind of demonstration You've got to be able to get George to picture it.

'Imagine, George, up there, you and I are like on a boundary between two dimensions. We're skimming, like dragonflies on the surface of a lake, but it's a vertical lake…'

'Dragonflies?'

'That's right. Skimming.'

'A vertical lake?' I held up my finger-tips as if I were touching the surface of some body of water above my head, and then brought the whole thing gingerly round to the vertical. 'Like this……'

'Gordon, I'm not stupid. I see what you mean.'

'Right then. So we nudge our cradles gently with our feet, keeping them swinging like pendulums. First swing: dampen the surface, second swing: skim off the smoky dust particles, the smears of bird lime that make up the microcosmic layer between glass and outside air. Third swing: dry off the damp smudge, and on last return swing, give it a bit of a shine. The whole process governed by the pendulum principle. The pristine result, George, is a sheet of glass which gives us a unique access to the two worlds. The one inside…hazy, closed off, …although apparently you managed to catch sight of the girl with the short skirt …. the other is the reflection of the world behind us. Do you see?'

'You do rabbit on, Gordon, don't you?'

'It's one of the things that goes with Philosophy,' I say lamely.

So here we are, a few hours later, on the same building but a bit further along. It's one of those days when the sky's full of great mountains of cumulus cloud with blue between. The window is all reflection. Beneath those cloud mountains there are roof tops, a swirl of pigeons, a tower block of offices bristling with aerials and housing for elevators and air-conditioners, even the upper deck of a green double-decker slides by with people staring at us, transfixed by the pendulum of our window cleaning. Then there is the spire of St. Peter's Church, and you may even catch a glimpse of the castle. It's like some twentieth century Bayeaux Tapestry. Or even a symphony. And it's full of sounds too, the chime of a tram's bell, a police siren, even the cry of a sea-gull, above the general hum of the traffic and people's shoes on the pavements.

Of course, on a day like this, if you tried to look through the glass, inside, well you would hardly see a thing, no more than you can see fish under the water in a canal..

I have to explain of course. There are different days. When the weather's dull it all changes and you can peer inwards through that smoked glass at the outlines of people at work:

clerks, cleaners, tea-ladies, senior executives, managers, whatever, all going about their affairs. But it's all indistinct & unreachable. Some are sitting down, some engrossed in papers or a screen, or on the phone, or in discussion, their arms folded. Others are bustling about. I've no idea what they're doing. Some even stand and stare out at the sky, but not as if they're seeing anything there. Funny really, they never seem to be aware that we're floating outside there. They may be just deep in thought perhaps, or in their own private worlds. George on the other hand tries to make out he has some kind of contact with them. He'll be telling us next that the girl in the short skirt waved back at him. And yet I know they never do.

I've noticed that the people inside appear not to communicate with each other properly. Their mouths move, they make gestures with their coffee cups, they might even frown or smile, you can't really be sure. They perch on the edge of each other's desks and scratch their heads, or push the hair away from their eyes. Only occasionally does someone, just for a second, send a fleeting glance at us in our cradles doing the pendulum thing. Even then they never look straight at us, although we are the ones engineering the whole operation. Perhaps they find us too embarrassing. Like they're staring at the belly of an insect, full-frontal, stuck there on the lake surface above them.

So for me and George, two worlds; the mysterious blue-grey silent film depths of those work stations and then, the joyous and uninhibited symphony of sky and cityscape in reflection behind us. Odd how George still prefers that inner world, and me the outer one.

But on this day precisely, George's view gets him into trouble.

Suddenly as I look across at him swinging on his cradle I can see he's trying to signal something to me. He looks upset about something. When we get down back to ground level he takes me to one side, away from the others.

'Did you see that? I could hardly believe my eyes!'

'What George?'

'That girl on the fifth.'

'Now, you said fourth floor before.'

'No, no, not that one. This one was higher up. You would have been able to see what I mean…you was better placed than me.'

'Well George I saw nothing. No one could see a thing. Look, it was sunny, George. It was all reflection.'

'There was just that moment when clouds went across…' 'So, what did you see?'

'I saw her, and then him. He assaulted her.'

'You what?'

'She was sitting at her desk, and then this man came in, looked like the boss, quite a bit older than her, and made her help him carry some boxes behind a partition, and then he….did it.'

'Did what, George?'

'He took hold of her, and pushed her against a cabinet, and then tried to pull up her dress..'

'Now look, George. What are you saying, mate? I mean, You shouldn't be looking….and it might have just been a bit of fun.'

'No way, Gordon. She was struggling, and she screamed out.'

'Now George, you couldn't have heard that…'

'No, but I could see it…I could see her mouth, and the dress all rucked up.'

'What happened then?'

'She pushed him off, then went off to the toilets. The man went back to his desk.'

'And nobody saw all this or said anything.'

'I told you Gordon. I saw it all…'

'I mean anyone inside.'

'There was no one else there. I suppose everyone else had gone off for lunch.'

We sit then for a few minutes. I'm speechless. First of all I'm convinced it isn't one of those days when anyone, even x-ray eyes George could have see what's going on inside. Even on a dull day, it isn't easy, but today is all sun. It must be just…George's imagination.

'Was she pretty George?'

'What the bloody hell has that got to do with it? She was, I admit she was. And I would recognise her again. But you're trying to insinuate that…'

'No George, I didn't mean that. It's just that you say you saw the outlines of people, sort of flickering, moving about, you could have…'

'Gordon. I saw it all. Don't give me any of that flickering stuff. Like I'd made it up. Or imagined it. It's nothing like that bird with the short skirt on the fourth floor….'

'So you made that up…'

'Some of it. I mean, you have to do something to liven things up a bit don't you. But not this time. This was real.'

I can see that it's going to be difficult to dislodge George from this fantasy, if it is a fantasy.

'Well,' I say finally, 'there's nothing we can do about it'. George says nothing. Just looks down at his sandwiches, as if he's only just noticed what he's eating.

'There is,' he says.

'Is what?'

'Something we can do.'

'What?'

'We finish at five don't we. Well I'm going to wait outside the entrance. And I shall tell the girl.'

'For God's sake, tell her what?'

'That I saw it all, and I would be willing to testify.'

I think this is the moment when I realise that things are getting out of control. Deep water stuff. I don't know what to say.

'You'd back me, wouldn't you Gordon?'

'But I didn't see anything George. How can I?'

'Well, I'll do it on my own then.' And he throws his sandwiches at the side of the hut and stalks off.

I don't get chance to talk to George again until we're finishing off. I 'm thinking he'll have cooled down and decided to let things alone. I couldn't have been more wrong. I'm still sorting my gear out when he's behind me again.. 'Are you going to back me then?'

'Look George, how can I? I didn't see a thing.'

'My imagination eh?'

'I don't know George but….'

But he cuts me off, turning abruptly and marches towards the building entrance. People are streaming out and it's about a minute before I can catch George up. But I'm too late. He's there with his back to me, facing this girl. I can see her face. She's pretty, with sharp features, brown hair, quite tall, but I guess reserved. She's colouring up and glancing nervously towards the main doors, as if she's more scared of who might come out of them, not of George's words whatever they are. Mind you, you can see she doesn't want to hear what George is telling her either. But she's not outraged or angry with him. When I arrive she just brushes past us. Saying nothing, but shaking her head. As if to say, I don't want to discuss any of it.

George is jubilant. As we go back to collect our gear, he tells me that he told her what he's seen and would be willing to 'testify'.

'And what did she say?'

'Nothing. No words. But you could tell she knew what I was on about.'

'Well she's gone now. That'll be the end of it.'

George just grunts.

'You're going to leave it now, aren't you?'

'For the time being. But I said I'd be there at the end of work tomorrow. Same time. Time for her to think about it. Consider her options.'

'George, George,' I said. 'It's all so…vague…'

'You mean, it's my imagination? I don't think so. Did you see her face when I told her?'

I didn't say a thing, I had to admit that George might be onto something. I'm angry though. George trying to drag me into his murky unreliable world. Can't he leave me alone with my nicely sunlit detached one.

'Watch out for a black eye if the boy-friend turns up,' I tell him.

We are not working on the same building the next day, so George gets away five minutes early and hurries round to Pearsons Holdings and reluctantly I follow. The more I think about it, the more I'm convinced that George could not have seen what he says he saw. It just wasn't the right kind of day. 'If she says leave it…you back off, okay?' I tell him.

George says nothing.

As we come round the corner of the building we can see her waiting there.

'So,' George says to her. 'Have you thought about it? Me & my mate are willing to…' I have no time to protest at his including me….

'I want you to leave me alone,' she says, her voice hoarse, almost breathless.

'But we'll support you. We know it's embarrassing, but that bastard needs nailing.'

'You're talking nonsense,' she says. 'You didn't see anything. And if you don't leave me alone, I shall report you.' And then, oddly, she waits to see what George has to say. And for once George doesn't really know what to say.

'We was just trying to help.' She looks hard at him, then at me.

'Well you can best help by keeping your nose out of it. Otherwise I'll get the police onto you…' And with that she turns away and walks off swiftly in the direction of town. George stands there and says nothing. He looks rattled. And I don't suppose I quite know what to do with myself. George has got himself into a silly situation and I'm not convinced he's got any sense on his side. 'In future, keep your eyes on the clouds and the sky,' I say to him silently. Aloud I say: 'You did what you could George.' End of story, or so I thought.

We are just moving off when a guy in a suit comes over to us.

'Are you the window cleaners?' he asks, coolly enough.

George looks at the man. Then he pulls himself up to all the inches he can muster and says:

'That's us. Why?'

'It's just that one of the girls in my department has been complaining about you guys peeping and then harassing her after work.'

'Harassing? What we saw yesterday mate was a bit more than harassing.'

It is at this point I realise that this is George's key character, the man who is supposed to have assaulted the girl. He's as cool as cucumber, or is a good actor. 'You saw nothing,' he says. 'All I need to do is pick up the phone and get through to your bosses, and you'll be out of it. There must be rules, about window-cleaners peeping. And slander.'

'Go ahead,' says George. 'There's rules about what you do with your hands when you're with your female staff. Especially when you've got them trapped up against a filing cabinet.. Only you don't only lose your job, they put you inside.'

'Preposterous,' he says angrily, and turns sharply back to the main entrance.

'Now you've done it,' I say. 'Come on let's leg it, while we can.'

'No Gordon. Can't you see it. He's trying to frighten us. He's as scared as she was.'

And then he is coming out of the building again, clutching his brief case. I'm thinking, why didn't he have it with him when he came out before. He stops on the steps and beckons to us. 'Careful George,' I say. We saunter across.

'If we could have a word in the foyer,' he says, and shows us through the swing doors. He points to a desk and chairs that are some way down a corridor. It doesn't really look like a trap, but I'm very wary. George by contrast looks confident.

He points to the chairs and we sit down.

'So you intend to pursue this ridiculous line of accusations?' I'm just on the brink of intervening, telling him that we....note, we, not George on his own...have made a big mistake, when he opens up the brief case and takes out a large envelope.

'Look how much do you two earn in a week?'

'What's that got to do with anything,' says George, almost triumphantly.

The man is looking uncomfortable, undecided. Then he says an odd thing.

'Well I suppose you're both men of the world?' I try to think what world he's talking about....George's inside world or my outside one, until I realise that he is implying something quite different.

'Here,' the man says, 'this should be enough, enough to....' And he stuffs the envelope into George's hand. He snaps the brief case shut and walks off out of the building like a man who has completed a successful business deal.

George slides the contents from the envelope. For a moment I think it's going to be a note or a confession or something. Then I see that it's money Twenty pound notes. A whole wadge of them. George begins to count them but when he's counted up to fifty he stops He hasn't got to half way. We both of us look at the money. Speechless. Then George slides it back inside the envelope.

'What'll you do with it?' I say

'We could take it to the police,' he says. 'Window cleaners don't earn this kind of money.'

'But we don't know whether the girl wants us to do this. We have to keep that in mind.'

'I suppose we could ask her,' says George. 'Or perhaps,' he says as if just inspired, 'we split it …sort of two ways. Half for her, and the other half you and I share. How about that?'

'I don't know,' I say. 'I don't like the look of that guy in the suit. It could go all wrong…. We'd all end up as…blackmailers or conspirators.'

'But he came and gave the money to us…we didn't put any pressure on him.'

'That's not the way he would make it look.'

'I suppose not. What should we do then? You think of something Gordon.'

'Thanks a lot.'

It's the next day before I'm able to talk to George about it again.

'You have to speak to the girl. See whether she's prepared…'

'I already have.'

'What?'

'I arranged to meet her last night. We went to the Bell.'

'She didn't mind us….interfering?

'Not when I explained. About the money. In fact, she seemed to think it a real laugh that we'd got that kind of money out of the skinflint of a boss.'

'So she wants us to go to the police with it?'

'No chance. Keep the money and shut up she says.'

'So you gave it her.'

'She took it like a shot. Here's your share,' and he hands me an envelope.

So that was that. £2000. It didn't seem quite right but I put it into my Building Society account.

Strange how an adventure like this sort of pushes George

and me together, and yet at the same time seems to thrust us apart. George is still the one for peering in through the windows, discreetly of course, and I get the impression he's now on the look-out for trouble, indiscretions, plots, so that he can mint something out of them. Of course he never does. But not through lack of imagination One day he comes to me and says he's seen some guy pouring over what looked like accounts, well at least figures, and carefully altering them. The man is sure to be on some kind of financial fiddle he says. Should he challenge the man, or send him a note. I tell him loud and clear to lay off, and that I will not support him in any more stunts like that.. He has been lucky on the one occasion…well three of us have been lucky…but lucky lightning didn't strike twice.

And for a week or so I see very little of George, and we even find ourselves working in different teams.

I put my share into the Building Society for a specific reason. Those days staring at the clouds and the sky, reflected in the windows, haven't been completely wasted. I've always fancied flying, you know, piloting an aeroplane. When I look into it, I find that really learning to fly, proper commercial aircraft, would cost me a lot more than £2000. So I'm going for lessons in gliding. Same clouds, same sky, less hurry. My only regret is that I can't fly over the city & Pearsons Holdings. They don't allow that. Reasonably enough.

Then after my sixth lesson, I meet George again in the Bell. He's at the bar collecting drinks. I try to tell him about my gliding, but he seems pre-occupied. Then he breaks with his news. He's with this girl, it is a long term steady thing. They are going to put the money down for a house. 'Come and have a word with Maureen…she's at that table there.'

We go over to where she's sitting. She looks up & I must say that it's a smirk she gives me as she says: 'Hallo Gordon. Remember me.'

Of course it is her. I hardly know what to say. I listen while they babble on, almost oblivious of me. Something about she's been to the Building Society and they'll let them have a mortgage on the property they are looking at out at Arnold. Luckily the £4000 is exactly the 5% deposit needed. I manage to interrupt them to say that I couldn't stay and I get up to go.' We'll invite you to the house-warming, won't we Georgy,' she says. 'When we've got a better idea of the date…'

'I might fly in,' I say flippantly. George looks as mystified as she does.

I'm standing by their table, ready to go, when Maureen catches hold of the bottom of my coat, and looks up at me. 'Gordon, before you go, I want to say one thing. Thank you for backing Gordon up over that whole thing. And persuading him not to go to the police. What good would that have done? Where would we be now if ….you know. As it is, things have turned out just right for all of us.'

I try to avoid George's eye.

'And you put that money on one side. You might find someone you fancy…'

'Oh I already have,' I said.

Her eyes light up. 'Good for you,' she says. 'What's her name?'

'Seagull,' I say and laugh. George still looks as mystified as she does so I leave them to try and work it out between them.

FALSE ALARMS

It was when he smoothed back the thin strips of hair above his ears that I recognised him. It wasn't the hair itself, which had been darker, more bushy then. Nor the face. No, it was the mannerism, deft, self-congratulatory. When he had started speaking, I felt I knew his face from somewhere, but after fifteen minutes it was the movement that gave things away. It was Thompson.

He certainly was at home on the Council benches. Pleasantly persuasive. Probably prepared to do a bit of bullying if it was called for. I'd been called in to advise on a legal matter. It had not occurred to me that Thompson might be here, forty years on. I heard the words 'developmental increments' and then the dreaded local authority jargon that year: 'additionality'. Thompson, the gang leader, still with that gift for words! I looked round the chamber. Perhaps scruffy Col would be here too, and even May with the milk chocolates. But most of the faces round me were stern with genuine or pretended concentration. A few of the old guard who had seen and heard it all before, sat with eyes closed, brazenly advertising their boredom. I sat and waited, suddenly aware that I didn't want to catch Thompson's eye.

* * *

It had all started when I overheard the angry buzz of conversation between my mum and dad in the kitchen. I turned the TV sound down.

'That's not the point Lill. This was deliberate, a malicious call. And now it's my mate Charlie that's in trouble.'

'The police'll sort it out love.'

'Fat chance! I reckon it's a gang of them.'

Dad was a fireman. The fire-station was just down the road. We would rush out when we heard the bells and sometimes catch a glimpse of him. He always referred to the fire-engines as 'machines'. I drew a picture of one at school and had to put the teacher right when she called it an 'engine'. They were 'machines', unless you were being fussy, then they were pump escapes, turntables ladders or emergency tenders. Anyway, there were traffic lights on the corner and the machines would edge up on them on red and then slide through, all careful. Even in emergencies they weren't allowed to break the rules, not just any old how, Dad said. Apparently on this occasion they had hit a car, which Charlie, the driver, would have to answer for. And in the end the call-out was a malicious one.

'It's their parents I blame,' said my mum.

'Them or their parents, I couldn't care which. I'd like to get my hands on them.'

Although I didn't understand the word 'malicious' I didn't like the sound of it. But it was the other thing that Dad said that worried me more …'a gang of them.' Because I belonged to a gang, well, a sort of gang. In fact I sort of belonged to it. There were four of us, all from the top juniors; we met on the wasteland by the railway on our way home from school. There was always a lot of rubble that could be heaved around, bottles smashed, even small fires to be lit. Of course I never mentioned the gang at home. If I got dirtier than usual, I said I'd been watching the trains.

Thompson was the boss. He was more worldly-wise than

anyone else I knew at school. He 'had been in trouble' with the police, he told us and was 'on their files'. I never knew his Christian name and he never allowed anyone to shorten his name to Tomo or anything. He had shortish hair which somehow dropped over his ears, hence the mannerism.

May, Thompson's girl friend, was the token female and exempt from the two rules of membership. To compensate for this she supplied us with chocolates and bourbon biscuits.

The third member of the gang, Col, thought he was very tough. He despised any form of cleanliness or neatness. A handed-down jumper in reasonable condition had to be 'worked over' to reduce it to the required level of shabbiness. He certainly despised me and kept inventing little challenges …bet you can't jump off this wall, bet you can't bend this piece of piping, bet you daren't do this or that. In a stand-up fight he could have demolished Thompson in seconds, but Thompson was too clever to let it come to that. In fact Col was in awe of him and I suppose we all were.

The first rule of membership was the committing of crimes. A crime was defined as any action that could get you into trouble with officials, shopkeepers, private citizens, or the police. Trouble with teachers or parents was automatically ruled out. Typical offences were knocking on doors, upsetting dustbins, visible and noisy damage to derelict buildings, chalking of rude words onto the railway bridge. I didn't have much courage for these exploits but desperately wanted to be a member of the gang. I suppose I was on probation.

My own choice of initiation offence had been an inspired one. It had been a hot day and we had been picking up globules of tar from the road and moulding them into balls. Col sucked his like a sweet. I suggested we push the balls into the front door locks of several houses. We were able to watch from an entry as more than one returning housewife struggled with shopping, pram, and a useless key. Thompson had been truly impressed. 'Shows intelligence,' he had said and I felt the warmth of acceptance. Thompson never said that about any of Col's escapades.

The second rule of membership was the regular use of the word 'fragging'. Thompson had selected the word after visiting the public library to consult a dictionary of slang. The word was not to be found there.

'If it'int in the dictionary, it can't be a swear word,' said Col.

'They daren't put it in, stupid.'

'Why not?'

'It's just too bad a word …they'd be in the courts for indecency. The book'd be withdrawn.'

'But what does 'fragging' mean?' said Col, still not completely satisfied.

'If you don't know, you wouldn't be able to understand even if I told you,' said Thompson with a sneer.

A few days' after the accident involving my Dad's mate, the four of us were sitting under the warehouse steps, vaguely planning our next crime.

'So, what are we going to fragging smash up today?' said Col. 'Why do we always have to smash things?' said Thompson nobly. 'Couldn't we do something more s'fisticated? Any ideas Dave?'

But Col interrupted. 'Why don't we call the fire brigade. Pretend there's a fire?'

A malicious call! The words themselves froze the blood in

my veins and I couldn't think sensibly about it. The person at the other end of that call could well be my father.

'What about it, Dave?' said Thompson

'What? Is it my turn?'

'Yeh!' he said. ''Bout time you did something. Col did that wall in opposite the shop yesterday.'

I took the plunge. 'The trouble is,' I said, trying not to catch his eye, 'I think it's a brilliant idea but there's two problems…'

'First, you're too fragging scared, second, you fragging daren't!' said Col.

'No, I'm not. It's just that…with my dad being in the fire-brigade, if I was caught, they'd send me to him. For him to… fragging… deal with. So that's not a real crime. By our rules.' 'But they wouldn't send you to him…'

'They fragging would. I heard my dad saying that he knew how he'd deal with them. They're called the malicious ones. So there!'

Both of them were looking at me, weighing up me up. I had to move fast.

'Look,' I said. 'I've got a much better idea. They've put up some new posters next to the railway bridge…..'

They followed me to the spot.

'Yours this one, Dave,' said Thompson.

I edged a finger nail under the bottom edge and began to pull. A narrow strip came away, right through a woman's smiling toothpasty mouth. Very effective…much worse than removing the whole poster. Then I had a go at a poster about an ice-hockey match then ripped a thin slice out of a foaming pint of beer, and was just starting on one of my favourites…a smirking pig pulling a pile of sausages with the caption **DRAWING HIS OWN CONCLUSION**…when….

'Well, well, David Enright. Who would have thought? Enjoying yourself?'

I turned, my knees like jelly. I first saw a policeman, then recognised him from the combined Policemen's and Firemen's Christmas Party.

'Your dad will be pleased, won't he?'

The others watched open-mouthed as I was led away.

First I was taken to my mum. She was horror-struck. Then in the evening I had to confess it all again in front of my dad. 'What on earth made you do that, David?'

'I don't know…it was a sort of accident…' I began.

Then he blew up. 'You lying little twerp,' he said. 'Accidental! You must think I've the brains of a blackclog beetle. To think that a son of mine….' And there was an unbearable contempt in his voice, and I realised that what had seemed so daring to me was to him contemptible. He was ashamed of me. I felt like shouting out; 'What if I'd called the fire brigade? If I'd done a malicious thingummy?' I almost felt he would have been even more angry, but at the same time have thought more of me in a funny sort of way. Then he belted me several times. I don't remember whether it hurt.

'Who else was with you?' my mum asked. I said there was no one. 'Well, I'll be meeting you at the school gate tomorrow,' my mum said grimly. It was almost the worst part of it. Luckily the other three were nowhere in sight when she came up and gripped me by the arm, but there were plenty of others to snigger.

When I eventually got to speak to Col and Thompson I was surprised how cowed they seemed.

'Did they take you in?' asked Col nervously.

'Sort of,' I said, with a trace of nonchalance.

'How many of them were there?'

'Three,' I said truthfully.

'Did they cross-question you? With lights?'

'The light were quite bright,' I said as I thought of our front room. 'Actually they talked about a gang.'

'You didn't snitch on us,' said Thompson, apprehensive.

'Trust me,' I said magnanimously.

From then on Thompson and Col seemed to avoid me, though May come up to me once, her eyes full of almond whirls and something else. Later that summer each of us went off to our secondary schools and we lost contact altogether.

* * *

Over on the opposite bench Thompson was still rattling on. I thought about the little nub of guilt I had been carrying about with me all these years and at its centre that moment of contempt, almost of rejection. My dad had never mentioned the incident again. And what I had eventually achieved over the years was something he had been proud of as far as I could tell. But it had always left me a bit wary of him. Even now when he was in his eighties.

Someone was asking Thompson a question about the legal position.

'I'm sure Mr Enright would be the best person to advise us here… the legal niceties are his province,' said the chairman. I rose to my feet, coaxing from the papers in front of me the necessary words Mostly of duplicity and avoidance. But before I spoke I looked up at Thompson, and then pointedly across the chamber to the fire alarm on the wall above the door. Thompson followed my gaze. Then looked back at me, obviously puzzled, not making any connections.

Perhaps my dad would have understood better.

NIGHT SONG OF THE B17 BANKER

In the early nineteen fifties I worked in the summer holidays as a porter on Victoria Station. In those days it was an impressively spacious though underused station of twelve platforms, down below road level, with tunnels at either end. And of course the still familiar clock tower. If you park your car today at the bottom level of the Victoria Centre underground car park you are on a level with the old tracks. There were fast trains to Sheffield and Newcastle, Leicester and London, and local trains to Grantham and to the coal mining towns of North Nottinghamshire.

The most memorable part of it all was being on the night shift. The main services stopped before midnight, and then over the next five hours there were just two night trains and a trail of freight trains until the first real train of the next day, the newspaper train from London. It was all steam, with B1s and B2s and occasional B17's 4-6.0s on express trains, sometimes even a 2-6.0 V2 and once in blue moon, a Gresley A3. I quote the numbers, but it is a long time ago, and could well be inaccurate. The station was like a huge empty but well-lit auditorium. And there was nothing for us to do. Occasionally the foreman would get us to sweep the stairs and platforms…a pointless exercise as the dust blew up off the tracks as fast as we swept, and I don't remember very much litter. After that, I would wander the platforms, occasionally kick a football made of old rags about and watch the unblinking signals at the entrance to the tunnels. Others more sensibly found themselves a corner of a coach, or one of the waiting rooms, to read a newspaper, or doze off.

Any tour of the station took me eventually to a siding in the centre of the station where the spare engine was 'parked'. It was kept 'in steam' in order to help banking freight trains out at the north end, or in case of a mechanical failure, to replace one of the night trains. I never saw it undertake either of these tasks. However what was most memorable about it, was its song. Throughout the night it kept up a background of sizzling and bubbling accompanied by bewitching sighs and whistles and esoteric crooning, a sort of plaintive night-music of brooding regret and expectation.

At four o-clock four of us, two regular porters and two students, made our way through the silent empty city, walking in the centre of the road, across Parliament Street, down Kings Street to Slab Square, down Wheeler Gate, past the Fountain and on to Arkwright St, (there being no Broad Marsh Centre in our way), by the Midland Station, and eventually to a downtown local station in the Meadows. Here at five the newspaper train arrived from London, and we were suddenly galvanised into ten minutes of hard work as the bundles of newspapers were heaved off the vans onto trolleys to be taken down to the waiting newsagents vans. The bundles were heavy, the binding twine rough, so for the students like myself it was painful work.

Then we rode the train into Victoria, skimming slowly with frequent halts over the Meadows. I think I have never seen anything so beautiful as those dawn visions of a city just at the point of awakening. Backyards, gardens, an occasional warehouse or workshop were suffused by that peculiarly delicate and innocent light of early morning. People could be seen standing at doorways, stretching themselves, dogs were making their first tour of the garden, the occasional early trolley bus trundled by.

Everywhere there was a sense of something new, untarnished unfolding. We passed over the Midland Station, through the complex of Boots and other factories, before plunging into the tunnel beneath High Pavement at Weekday Cross. That bit of the journey, without the tunnel, can be relived by anyone today travelling by tram from the station to the city centre.

At Victoria Station again, there was another arduous unloading to be done, before we could slope off home. And then I would wonder as always after the long hours of the night shift, how to use a day which was so obviously alive, full of potential. It seemed wrong to go home to sleep. One answer was to sit with the early morning taxi and bus drivers at the café on Parliament Street, and if one had the cash, eat a toasted bacon sandwich and a mug of tea. At home sleep did not come for me until early in the afternoon, and then when I awoke, it was dark again and time to get off to Victoria for the next night shift.

ROCKS IN A LANDSCAPE

Tom parked his car in the yard and looked across at the house. 'A lot of clearing out to be done,' he told himself. 'And not before time.'

He went in and put the kettle on for a cup of tea, and then with deliberate carefulness took down a china cup and saucer from the cabinet. He heard his grandfather's whining voice: 'Only poofters drink out of that daft china. Proper tea comes in a mug.' Tom turned to the chair expecting to see the old man there. 'We only drink out of them when there's a funeral,' he'd have said. Well, what better opportunity, Tom thought. There had been a funeral …his grandfather's. He could drink out of whatever cup he liked now. No-one to stop him. Least of all his grandfather.

They had buried him in the cemetery in the town that morning. A dozen or so neighbours, relatives had come to the service and some had stayed on at his Mother's house for sandwiches, cake and cups of tea. The tiny front room was full of relatives, neighbours and forced cheerfulness. Someone carelessly remarked that they thought grandfather had died a few years back. Then there was Tom's uncle, a prosperous business man from the south, who puffed and sweated, and made everyone feel as uncomfortable as he was.

'You'll miss the old fellow,' he said to Tom breezily.

There was silence.

'We all will,' a neighbour added, less confident.

'I suppose so,' Tom had said. And the conversation had moved on to the weather.

When the visitors had gone, he helped his mother with the

washing-up. She seemed strangely unmoved by her father's death. It was as if she and her father had made some kind of contractual farewell many years before. In any case she had Tom's younger brother and sister to look after, as well as an invalid husband. There was a job at the local hospital to supplement the meagre pension from the firm where Tom's father had worked, before the accident.

'You might as well stay on,' she said. 'In Grandad's house. That's if you don't mind. It'll be ages before it is sold, so you stay on until your course is finished. You know you can always come here, for a meal, any time.'

'I'll be okay mam.'

'If you really wanted to you could come back here. We could make room somehow. It's just that there's no space for all your stuff….'

'I know mam, I know. The farm will suit me fine. You've got enough on your plate here. I'm not going to be much help.' 'You don't mind being on your own then?' He shook his head. How could be explain to his mother that he was looking forward to the freedom without her dad there.

He went into the front room where his own dad was still sitting, waiting to be moved back into the kitchen.

'I'll be getting back then,' he said.

His Dad just smiled, as if he understood. Difficult to know what to do for the best, the way his dad was so shut off from things. Just a smile and a pat on the shoulder was all he could muster.

When he first moved in with his grandfather over a year ago his Mother had said: 'You aren't expected to nurse him, you know. He wouldn't let you anyway; you know what's he's like,

It's just so there's someone around should he need help.'

'It's okay Mam. I'll manage.'

'I feel awful ....dumping him on you. I know how difficult he can be. Promise you'll say if it's not working out.'

'I promise mam.'

'You know, he wasn't always as difficult. He worked very hard, too hard, and then when he had to stop he couldn't seem to settle. Especially when the arthritis got him. So you have to make allowances.'

'Yes mam.'

Because it was convenient in many ways. A room upstairs of his own and another one downstairs that he could use as a dark-room, all rent free. And garage space too. It was an old farmhouse, most of its outbuildings having been demolished. The farm work had ceased twenty years ago. It was never quite clear what this had involved for grandad. This was the last house outside the village on a narrow road which zigzagged up onto the moor. For Tom it was only a half-hour's drive down into the next town for the college. The arrangement was nearly ideal. And all in exchange for keeping a watchful eye on grandfather, doing his shopping, collecting medicines. Nothing to it really. The old man wasn't ill except for arthritis. He could struggle across the yard to the gate, when it wasn't too windy or cold, and lean on the fence to look out over the moor. At first he would even make the half mile to the White Lion in the village for a drink. That was becoming more difficult, and he refused Tom's offer of a lift. Didn't want to make a nuisance of himself. 'No one there I know,' he would say. 'New people behind the bar. And some of the customers. Snobby lot.' Mostly he stayed perched on a torn and evil-smelling old armchair, muttering to himself, smoothing a grey slick of hair over his bald head, or silent, his mouth partly open. He watched television, read the local paper from cover to cover, ate untidily and absentmindedly, and slept in snatches.

There were times however, perhaps over a meal, or watching television, when Tom could feel himself coming under observation…and being weighed up. And definitely found wanting, he thought with a shrug. At nine the old man went off to bed. He came down for breakfast just before Tom went off to the college. Tom left the house with the smell of grubby pyjamas and old age in his nostrils.

The disapproval was more clearly confirmed eventually 'So, you all sorted out at that college then,' his grandad said over one of their meals.

It was difficult to know how to answer.

'I mean, ready to get cracking with the old camera,' he went on, peering over the top of a slice of bread folded over several chips laden with ketchup, his mouth open, waiting for a reply.

'There's a lot of technical stuff to learn. Before you can really start taking pictures.'

'I know, I know,' the old man said tetchily. 'Still two years, I mean, they drag it out a bit, don't they?' Then the bread and chips were rammed home.

Tom went on to explain about getting his portfolio together. 'So,' his granddad said, chomping bread and ketchup, 'you won't be straight on to weddings and that kind of thing…'

'I have to prepare pictures for an exhibition.'

'How do you mean?'

Tom picked up an expensive book of pictures by a well-known photographer. Black and white views of city street corners, churches, monuments, old pubs, parks. He tried to keep the pages away from the greasy armchair.

'But these 'ere pictures must be fakes,' his grandad said.

'Fakes?'

'Nobody on them. Hardly any cars. Daft if you ask me. Makes no sense. In the middle of London! How do they do it… blot them all out?'

'The photographer didn't want people on them. He chose the buildings, the architecture, the shadows on the stonework, that sort of thing. Probably shot them in the early hours before anyone was about.'

'Unnatural if you ask me. Mind you, I wouldn't know. Sort of old fashioned too.'

'Old fashioned?'

'All black and white. Still if it's what you're supposed to do. Seems a bit arty-farty to me. Not my business of course.' Then after a pause. 'Any money in it?'

'Not for a few years.'

'Why ever not? You no good at it then?'

'Look Grandad I've got to establish a distinctive style.'

'Daft if you ask me. If it were me, I'd say get onto Weddings. Or what about them pictures they tek from aeroplanes. Hydro-electric Dams, the Colorado Canyon, the 'Ouses of Parliament. What about the Boat Race, like on the telly?'

'Grandad. I've just got to concentrate on my portfolio. Twenty good local pictures.'

'Of what? Round here? Views like?'

'Anything. Could be people, animals, buildings, the moors…

'Now that it'd be summat like. How about a badger…or a fox getting a bloody rabbit.' He was well into a huge wedge of apple pie that was in danger of dislodging his dental plate. 'Or pin-up pictures of gels. Like the ones in the newspapers.'

And then Tom stormed out, his own meal unfinished and his grandfather's wheezing baked-apple words in his ears, the sensation of long silky-hard fingers rubbing crumbs away on the side of the armchair. There were many other days when they rubbed up against each other. He told himself that he didn't care what his grandad said or thought of him, but the persistent disapproval wormed into him, like a slow fever.

With some trepidation he brought Beth his girl friend to see his grandfather on one occasion. She was a year older than Tom, doing a Design course at the same College. Her confidence was a constant surprise to Tom. Not only was she attractive and popular, but she took her studies in her stride and got on with people, her enthusiasm out in the open. Tom had never been very sociable. He supposed that it had been Beth who had initiated the friendship. He had only been going out with her for a month and in some ways was not sure what his relationship with her amounted to. But with grandfather she was immediately comfortable, coaxing him, teasing him, not in the least put out by his grubbiness and occasional coarseness. Only on one occasion did Grandfather give him that old leering look, and a wink in Tom's direction. The subject of Tom's portfolio had been raised and Beth herself had mentioned the need to make it attractive. Tom hoped that Beth had no inkling of what the wink was implying.

Later on the way home, Beth talked about his grandfather. 'He's a nice old man. Just lonely probably. How long since his wife died?'

'Oh about five years I should think.'

'He just needs cheering up a bit. Spoiling.'

'Well I wish I knew how I could do that.'

'I'm sure he's grateful, having you around.'

'He certainly doesn't show it. He's always… critical. Difficult to please.'

'You have to make allowance for his age.'

'I suppose so.'

After a pause, she went on.

'You know it's probably wrong of me to say this……'

'Go on.'

'Well he reminds me of you, in some ways.'

'Come off it!' horrified.

'No, I don't mean it in the wrong way.'

'I should hope not. I can't think of a single way…'

'No, Tom it's just the sort of, I don't know, dogged way you go at things.'

'Dogged? Is that a compliment?'

'Of course it is. I bet your granddad was just the same when he was younger.'

'Well, my mum always said he had a reputation for being a hard worker.'

'There you go then.'

''Dogged' still sounds a funny word to me…..like determined but…'

'Not enjoying it as much as you ought to.'

'Enjoying it doesn't quite seem to right word for it.'

'But I can see how much it all means to you, your pictures. No one's denying your commitment. Just…why not have a bit more fun with it.'

'Well, I'll see what I can do,' sarcastically. 'I'll hang some balloons out on the rocks, okay.'

'You know what I mean, Tom.'

'I don't really know whether I do Beth.'

'Anyhow don't worry about it.' Though of course he did. Then she laughed. 'What was that big wink he gave you?'

'Oh nothing,' said Tom blushing.

'Men's secrets eh? That has to be about women. Sex?'

Tom could find nothing else to say. When they got to her house she turned and kissed him and said: 'Don't worry. The secret is safe between you two. Remember to thank your granddad for having me. See you at the College tomorrow.'

Tom had spent several weeks in February and March going up onto the moor, photographing the group of rocks, the stream beds, old walls and fences, and stunted trees. He took his camera and some filters. In the evening he would work late into the night developing, selecting either clear or veiled lighting effects, enlarging close-up shots of pebbles or particular chunks of rock on the floor of a peaty stream. It was the hardness and permanence, even the static quality, of the landscape which he wanted to capture. The spiky blades of grass. The gritty rock surfaces with their scabs of lichen, the black secrecy of crevices. And overall the brooding sky with low clouds.

He found himself concentrating on the rocks which his grandfather called the Buttertubs, a group of grit-stone slabs high on the moors. It was a climb of over an hour. He had planned to photograph them against the snow, but this year there was none that persisted. He concentrated on early morning or evening sunlight touching the smooth beak-like edges of the slabs. Because he could walk right round them he could angle shots between the largest ones, so that their shapes were displayed like noses, earlobes, jawbones, foreheads, domed skulls and the folded limbs of recumbent figures.

He didn't allow any warmth or life into his pictures. Even if it had been summer he would have avoided shots of leafy bilberry or moorland flowers, coy and innocent against the slabs' harsh cragginess. As for lambs frolicking, young lovers wandering aimlessly across the grass, hair streaming in the wind, those were precisely the images that he wanted to avoid at all costs. He didn't even strive for romantic Wuthering Heights-style images, stormy clouds, isolated trees. In the darkroom he muzzed the edges, subduing any hint of scintillation. February was the ideal month for him. Hard lines, unyielding surfaces, a dampness that clamped down on the negatives and oozed from the grey and black exposures that emerged from the trays.

But in the end he was dissatisfied with what he was doing. There was some perspective that was missing which he couldn't identify.

He showed some of the pictures to his grandfather wondering in desperation whether his more jaundiced eye would light on what was missing. But he only peered at them and grunted, 'Ah, them Buttertubs.' He peered balefully at the black stones. 'Black,' he said, 'And weird. Like dead things. They allus was black of course….'

'That was the effect I was aiming at.'

'Dead. Like someone looking at his own skull in a mirror,' he said, baring his teeth almost into a snarl. 'Pity! Is that all could see in the place, lad? It warn't allus like that……I remember teking your ma when she were only a gel, and the lad …that snooty uncle o'yours, from London, up there. Lovely day it wore. See for miles. They collected flowers and we saw some rabbits. It were sunny and them slabs were warm, I remember just lying back on 'em with a fag, watching the kids larking about. The grass was all ruffled, like an eiderdown, it seemed to 'ave, you know, 'give' in it. And there was birds high up, wailing…' He stopped. Then the hardness came back into his voice: 'Not like that grass on them pictures of yours. More like bloody wire wool.' He turned back to Coronation Street. 'Terrible programme,' he would say afterwards.

'Why watch it then?

'There's nowt else on,' came the same old reply.

Then two weeks ago the old man had caught a cold, then pneumonia and had to be moved to hospital. Tom visited him there, dreading the meeting, anticipating that he would say something to shame him in the ward before the other patients and their visitors. But he'd changed. It was as if all that skirmishing in the farmhouse was his final act of some kind of protest. He seemed unnaturally calm and looked at Tom without rancour or watchfulness. 'Make sure you keep up with the photographs. And with that young lady,' he added with a wink. 'I didn't tell you. Used to tek pictures myself,' he muttered. 'Like you, up at the Buttertubs and all over there.'

'Pictures of what, Grandad?

'You'll see soon enough. Now I want you to make sure your mam gets them…'

'Sure. Where…do you keep them?'

But his Grandad had dozed off again. A week later he died with no sign of reluctance or protest.

And so now here he was with the clearing out to be done. For a start the armchair. He tried to drink his tea but the sound of his granddad's voice still hung in the air and the cracked mugs menaced him from the draining board. The smell of cold chips and mouldy apple hung over the kitchen. Thank goodness, his mother would be there on the next day to help clear things out, & above all to sort out his grandad's bedroom.

He went into the bedroom. From the window, on a clearer day, the Buttercubs were probably visible. He wondered about the photographs he had mentioned in hospital. He could find no camera, nor any kind of album. Under the medicine bottle by the bedside was an exercise book with tea stains on the cover. He presumed that was its function. Inside however there were twenty or thirty snapshots. All black and white, all faded ~~sometimes~~ to sepia. A stocky woman in her thirties was playing with two children. They smiled cheekily or coyly at the camera. They posed with little handfuls of berries, or sprigs of heather. The younger one, surely Tom's mother, was holding a tiny flower … one knew instinctively it was blue. In another picture the boy was pointing at the sky. Perhaps that apostrophe in the corner of the print was a bird, if not a hair on the lens.

He studied the picture of his mam and the uncle. In spite of the smallness of the pictures and the lack of definition, he couldn't help noticing the childrens' bonyness, all elbows, and knees. His Grandfather appeared on one picture only. He was sitting on one of the slabs with the girl on his knee, staring straight at the camera. He was grinning in a kind of triumph: 'See what a good time we're having.'

And then Tom looked through the photographs again. Of course they were faded, amateurish, the camera angled never quite right, the horizon crooked, the subject matter out of balance. But what he noticed now in the background was the way the Buttertubs appeared. The same shapes as on his own pictures, but no more than that, not menacing, just part of the backcloth. Without the photographer intending it, they gave definition to the lightness and happiness of the figures in the foreground. The bones showing through on the human figures accompanied the bones showing through the moorland landscape.

Tom walked back to the darkroom and looked at the displayed sequence of his own pictures on the wall. 'Arty-farty,' he heard his grandfather say behind him and turned with a gasp. But there was no one. Suddenly he lunged at the pictures, tore them from the wall and rushed back into the kitchen. He forced them all into the gaping holes of the armchair, and then dragged the chair out into the yard. A splash of petrol, a match and it went up like a torch. 'See how you like that, you old bugger,' he shouted almost in tears. There was a pungent smell of burning plastic. He added some garden rubbish and bits of wood to the pile so that a great cloud of smoke billowed out over the garden and onto the moor. Dragging on his anorak, he clambered over the wall and began to ascend to the dampness of the rocks.

'If the house gets burned down too, so be it. I couldn't care less,' he shouted back at the smoke which now hid the house from view. 'Good riddance.' But then at the last minute he remembered the exercise book. He rushed back up the stairs and retrieved it from the old man's bedside and pushed it into his anorak pocket.

Ten minutes later he looked back at the smoke, but now it was only a grey trickle, no danger to anyone. As he approached the grey rocks ahead of him, the mist cleared a little, and he saw again the anthropomorphic shapes, grotesque, unyielding. But behind them, and through the cracks and spaces, he saw crisp curves of moving light-filled particles of cloud, the sharp edges and plumes of distant cooling towers on the plains to the west. A moorland bird fluttered across the skyline and he heard its wailing, but no longer agonised, cry. And suddenly he saw the stones as they had appeared in his grandfather's snaps dropping into place. Mere anchors dropped on the moor ….the white holes on his negatives, points of rest, pivots for what really mattered: the lightness of the clouds, the warmth of the low bushes grass and heather, the space where children and adults moved and played.

So it seemed in the end that his grandfather had told him about himself, in his own very indirect way. He would have to give the photographs to his mother. He hoped once she had seen them that she would let him keep them. More important, he knew now what he had to do. He had, as his grandfather had said, to get 'cracking' with the camera. It would still be the slabs and moorland, because that was under his skin, part of the fabric of the landscape he wanted to photograph. But somehow he had to get people into the pictures. Not as a counterpoint to the megalithic quality of the slabs, or anything like that. Just so that the rocks and the people could share the landscape. He would bring them all up here, Mam, Dad too … it wouldn't be so difficult …his sister and brother. When it was a bit warmer they'd make a real day of it. And he would have his camera.

And Beth could come too. He had a fleeting glimpse of Beth sitting on the rocks, posing. Perhaps Grandfather had got something, even if he'd made it sound wrong. Just a plain but beautiful human figure, against the almost human rocks.

He wished he'd thought of it earlier. So that grandad could have been included in the trip. Even with his moans and grumbles. After all it was his photographs that had shed new light on things.

CHRISTINA

The question was, did she really need to know. In a moment they were going to tell her, and then she would no longer be the person she was now. She would become that person they would be telling her about. It might well be the one that inhabited the shadows of her life.

Clasping her finger closely she stared down at the geometrical design of the carpet. The seat she was sitting on was unyielding. The room, altogether neutral with its moss-green walls, heavy dark furniture, was clearly a place without a function. In the corner there was a group of almost colourless dried flowers in a vase. Although there were high windows, the room was overlooked by office blocks, and not much light was allowed in. It's not our regular waiting room, the receptionist had said rather sharply, almost as if it were Christine's fault. The corridor they had used to get there was lined with ladders, cloths, tins of emulsion, and the smell of turps.

But even here in this unfamiliar territory, thought Christine, the shadows were not empty. She was here: the other person, waiting, able to reach across and touch Christine's wrist, her shoulder. She thought she could hear even the light exhalation of her breathing.. Even the beat of a heart. In fact, did she hear a stifled snicker, almost of contempt. As if she were biding her time. Like she always did, in the dark end of a corridor, in the fresh-linen hush of the airing cupboard, or even in the scratching of the foliage in the garden. Waiting to ensnare her, to descend upon her like a shroud, to glide over her skin and soak into her body, penetrating her chest and abdomen, piercing her heart, lungs and brain. To claim her. Or perhaps to liberate? One couldn't quite be sure.

Christine aligned her right feet with the geometry of the carpet, one foot flat, the other twisted onto its edge. 'Keep turning your feet like that and they'll come to stick like it,' her mother used to say to her. Well, the person she always called mother. But she always did it anyhow. 'Now stop that at once,' said the person she called mother. 'Silly girl. Why do you have to be so difficult?' And that made her laugh, though not out loud. Because difficult was what they always found her. Someone who had not managed to come up to expectations. And yet how could you be sure what people, especially adoptive parents, wanted you to be. How can you be expected to put your feet flat down on the ground if you are not sure? Sure who you are. And sure of the ground you are standing on. She supposed that was the sort of thing the other woman, the one in the shadows, would know, and know for sure.

The door was opened and the receptionist peered in, and beckoned to her. She followed her pecking walk back along the corridor, squeezing by the decorators' equipment, and then another corridor at right angles until she was ushered into another room.

On entering her first reaction was to drop her head and shield her face. The room was full of the most extraordinary radiance. Two great picture windows filled the room with unimpeded light. No shadows, nowhere for anyone to hide. No unlit corners for anyone to lurk in, waiting to invade her or whatever. This was a place, she thought later on, where the light and the truth of things would be inextricably linked.

A person who was for her merely a silhouette rose from a desk.

'Miss Christina Birtle.....do sit down.'

She sat down on a chair at about forty-five degrees from the desk and now could look at the speaker properly. The top of his head with its wispy grey hair was backlit, like a halo. He had mentioned a name but she hardly heard it.. Now she could see too a woman sitting some way back from the desk, as if observing.

'Actually, it's Christine Birtle, not Christina,' Christine said faintly.'With an E.'

There was some shuffling of papers and clearing of the throat, a subdued whispering with the other woman, then: 'There's no doubt about it, Miss... er... Birtle. The name given by your ...natural mother, was Christina. With an A. Obviously some error, perhaps some adjustment has been made since then. But not to worry. It doesn't invalidate anything. No one is likely to make a fuss.'

'Oh but they should,' she almost said out loud. 'Should be fussy. Very fussy indeed.' She sat trying to make sense of her own thoughts. Because something had clicked. It was the name. Suddenly it was as if that dreaded figure, her doppelganger, was being deprived of air, fading away like mist. She suddenly knew with absolute confidence that the presence in the shadows had in any case been a sham, something her own brain had contrived to fill her with dread. Here in the light she was indeed Christina with an A. She could hear a woman, perhaps the one they had referred to as her natural mother, looking down at her, saying it. She could see her face, the arch of finely drawn eyebrows, the large almost colourless yet subtly kaleidoscopic eyes, hovering over her like openings into a firmament. And the texture of the skin on the cheeks, the lips. The fingers touching her cheek. And her smell!

She stood up. 'I think you've told me all I need to know,' she said. 'You've been most kind.'

'But there is rather more to discuss, Miss Birtle,' the man went on. 'Before we can arrange a meeting.' And his voice rumbled on and she answered with nods and shrugs hardly taking any of it in. There was a piece of paper. A name, an address, a date, the suggestion that the other woman in the room might accompany her. And then another sheet which the man was urging her to read. It was difficult to make sense of the words. 'After all,' she said too quietly for them to hear, 'I do now know who I am and that's all that matters.'

'I beg your pardon?'

She smiled at the man, suddenly aware of his kindness. 'Yes, I'll go and see her.'

'That will be fine, Miss Birtle. Your Mother …….has been informed of course and expressed a wish to see you. All the information is on the paper. But I must ask to read the rest of the document most carefully, and then if you have any questions Mrs Peters here will endeavour to answer them.' His voice droned on while Christina, with an A, unlocked her clasped fingers, and practised putting two feet squarely onto the ground. After all, the documents might say things she didn't particularly want to hear. But she would be able to deal with that in due course. Rediscovering that tenuous link with the person she really was, was the reality. The other things, her mother back at home, this new mother, all that would work itself out.

She descended to the street and strode resolutely towards a pelican crossing at the end of the busy road. The sun was hot on the road surface and the buildings cast hard shadows on the pavement. But she didn't dodge them …they held no fear for her. Because for the first time, she knew that no one was tailing her. At the crossing she pressed the button and almost immediately the traffic came to a halt. On the other side she walked into a shopping precinct and walked through, aloof, content, admiring the shop front displays. 'Retail therapy' they called it didn't they. What some people went for in order to fill some void, make up for a loss. Well, she Christina had no need of it. Quite alone, yet she had never felt so completely herself as she did now.

'Extraordinary young woman,' the man said to Mrs Peters when Christina had gone. 'I hope she was taking note of what I said.'

'She'll be okay,' said Mrs Peters. 'She'll decide what she wants to do. In her own time. Strange though. The way she sat up, made herself taller, when you mentioned the spelling of the name.'

'Yes, I noticed that,' he said as he turned to the next file. 'Almost as if there were some new responsibility in front of her. As indeed there is, of course.'

'But, I suspect, something she is looking forward to.'

FOOL'S GOLD

Nobody could have been more surprised than Peter Wood when he heard that Fool's Gold was on the short list of eight. But not to get him wrong …he was convinced what he had written was a stunner, might one day be deemed a classic, but he didn't think the critics and other people who read the books and made judgements for the rest of us would see it that way. And indeed he was right. Of the five reviews he had read, not one was complimentary. 'Pedestrian' said the Guardian. 'Excessively preoccupied with financial world' said the Independent. 'Boring' said the Mail. One of the others used the words 'pretentious crap'. None of this had prevented sales from being modestly brisk though no deluge. And when the short list came out, suddenly it seemed to Peter Wood that he might be getting, at long last, proper recognition.

Looking down the road from his own hotel, Peter could see the entrance of the more prepossessing hotel chosen for the Independent Crime Writers' Award ceremony. It was the sort of place for Ballroom Dancing competitions, minor party conferences that sort of thing. His own room was in a separate hotel close by, the Excelsior…he had booked in there himself to avoid too close a contact with what was about to be enacted. In an hour's time the final eight would be wined, dined and then told whether they had won or failed. The award was of course the thing to have; people said it made agents and their accountants more attentive. And to be honest, the writers coveted the award too ….well this one did. Though loath to admit it in public. Like all the eight writers, he would have said that the £10,000 prize was the main attraction.

However, the comments by those same papers when they saw Fool's Gold on the short list had been even more discouraging. None of them could understand how it got there. Whereas the other seven sported odds of 5 to 1, 10 to 1, 15 to1, Fool's Gold was quoted at 100 to 1. Not that you took much notice of these things, if you were real writer, like Peter!

The light was beginning to fade, the sun having just dipped into the sea in the far west. Time to go along to the main Hotel and face the music. How could anyone, thought Peter, enjoy this kind of event unless you were sure of winning. Give them their due, the meal was usually quite decent. But just sitting there, the interminable speeches and really awful crime-based jokes and innuendo, and the build-up to awards with the oohs and the ahs. Their might even be a television crew there, which meant the tedium of re-runs of hand-shakes and that sort of thing. And everyone smiling grimly through, even though a great wave of hatred ran though seven people's bodies as lucky X scrambled, all apologies and mock-humility, to the rostrum to collect the loot.

But did he have to go at all? Why inflict it upon himself? It was a lovely warm evening, the sea was calm, just a hint of the sun's redness on the crest of the waves. Down the road there would be an adequate fish and chip shop so that he could eat as he walked along the front. One hundred to one! Why waste a perfectly pleasant evening.

He leapt to his feet, threw aside his black jacket and bow tie, pulled his shirt tails out of his trousers, and went down to the hotel lobby.. On the front steps, he turned back and went over to the desk. Better to cover himself, he thought and wrote on a slip of paper: 'Staying at the Excelsior just down the road but have been called away. Be back by nine, should I be needed.' Then he took another piece of paper, and wrote the same, leaving out the final clause. He addressed the envelope to the Chairman and asked if someone at reception could deliver it to the main Hotel.

The walk along the beach sand soon cleared his head and the fish and chips were okay as long as you didn't linger. There were several couples taking the same walk as himself, along with two or three solitaries, mostly with their dogs. Peter found himself watching them all, taking a delight in the detail of their dress, their way of walking, wondering what stories were tucked away in their casual progress. This young couple; why was her face so serious, what was she explaining with such intent concentration to her partner. And the elderly couple, quite silent, but seeming almost to cling to each other, as if they had just survived some catastrophe. And that bald man with the dog, throwing stones into the water, as if he hated the sea. And the dog aloof from stones, sea and the man.

Of course once a writer, always a writer. Always the observer, and the fantasist. But not always. Or even, if he was to judge from his critics, had he ever been. Take this last novel, his seventh crime novel; no one every criticised his plots, so carefully worked out, but people did complain about the characters. Cardboard cut-outs from the criminal and police world, someone unkindly said. Perhaps it was time for him to go for a more literary style, a novel peopled with the kind of characters he had just seen walking the beach. The ups and downs of everyday life for ordinary folk, made memorable and enduring by the sheer quality of the writing.

It would of course be a big jump. Fool's Gold was about a

group of con men in the financial world. Masterminded by the enigmatic Pedr Holz the group had operated a huge fraud based on a network of so-called financial advisors and an international hotel group. The story moved from London to Rio, from New York to Milan, with a short episode in Hong Kong. Eventually the operation was rumbled: a careless word to his mistress by the latest initiate to the group picked up eventually by the amateur sleuth, an economics professor from a foreign university. The criminal fraud officers involved were always a thousand miles or a couple of days behind things. But even Peter had to admit that 'ordinary folk' hardly featured in his work; even the blabber's mistress was a fashion model.

He had walked for three-quarters of an hour, beyond even the end of the front. But it was so light that he hadn't felt the need to return. But he must. In fact, he realised that he would like to get back to his room. He could feel the new characters and the events beginning to come to life, to breathe, and to interact. That earnest look on the face of the girl; the elderly couple clinging to each other, the angry man with the dog …he wanted to get some of it down, while it was fresh in his memory.

As he stepped into the Excelsior's lobby, a man came forward, introducing himself as the manager. 'A man and a woman were here; they wanted to speak to you. An urgent matter, they said.'

'Did they say who they were?' he asked, with the faintest shiver of excitement.

'No Mr Wood. But they showed me your picture. On the back of a book.'

'They did, did they!' Peter was hardly able to breathe. He realised that his mouth was open.

Perhaps he should go up the road to the main Hotel. He hardly dared contemplate what these two had wanted him for, unless it was ......but surely not. But on the other hand why not? Perhaps in the end there were people that really did recognise quality and talent when they saw it. In the end he decided to stay put. 'Let them come to me. Better not show too much enthusiasm,' he thought.

'Please send them up to my room when they return,' he said to the manager.

The next quarter of an hour he paced his room, trying to cool down, to think sensibly about the possibilities. But in fact only one thing occupied his mind: the Award, and the ten thousand smackers, was his. Why else would they need to see him? Urgently. There were no second prizes, runners up or that sort of thing.

When the knock-on the door came however it made him jump. There was the manager, ushering in the man and woman before leaving with a bit of a flourish. Peter recognised the restrained suits of typical PR guys, the slightly reserved smile. If you had won a box of chocolates they would be all jovial, but £10,000...that required a very specially restrained kind of smile. And joy, oh joy. Each had a copy of Fool's Gold in their hands.

'Mr Wood. Mr Peter Wood.'

'That's right...'

'Of 12 Priory Gardens, Harrow.'

'Yes of course that's me,' he said, trying to nod conspiratorially towards the book in the man's hand. Strange, he noticed that the girl was hardly taking any notice of him. She just looked round the room, as if inventorying its contents. The dinner jacket thrown carelessly onto the bed, his suitcase open, the usual chaos of garments visible. And when she looked back at him, he realised she was doing the same for the clothes he was wearing., his hair, the rather foolish way he was waving his hands.

'Look come on,' he said. 'Well who won it then?'

They both looked at him coolly, then each passed over to him a small wallet and an identification card.

'Chief Inspector Middleton. And Sergeant Cork.' The man said. 'I wonder if we could have a word with you.'

For a moment, Peter Wood almost swooned as the wave of disappointment struck him, so much so that he didn't quite make sense of the Inspector's first words. Somehow he and the Chief Inspector sat down, the Sergeant stood by the door, He noticed that she continued to look at him. He wondered if his shirt collar was crooked, his shoes slightly soiled by the sand. He sensed that he was in some way being assessed.

Then a book was handed to him, his book, and he was asked to acknowledge that he was in fact the author. Then came the explanations.

'Over the last year, we have been investigating a series of what we believe to be fraudulent business deals, in a number of major cities, which involve so-called financial advisors & the staff of a hotel chain. At this point I'm not permitted to put a name to any of these. Your book, Mr Wood, has been presented to us as giving a sort of 'blue-print' for this kind of operation. We felt we ought to speak to you.'

'Well of course people copy what they see in books….I can't be held responsible for…..I ask you. Should Shakespeare be held responsible for Macbeth's regicide?'

'On the other hand,' said Sergeant Cork, sliding into the

conversation, in a way that Peter felt was slightly insolent, 'there could be other motivations'.

'I don't quite understand.'

'Vanity might mean that the cleverest fraudster would still like his story to be told.'

The Chief Inspector raised his hands in a dismissive gesture. 'Now Sergeant Cork. Let's not start using our imagination. I'm sorry Mr Wood, no one is making any kind of suppositions yet. We're just here to clear up a few details. The point is, Mr Wood, we've both studied your book very closely and have more or less come to the conclusion that it's all just a coincidence. In fact, if you are able to confirm that you were not in or near Milan on January 21st…'

Confused, Peter Wood picked up his diary from the open suitcase..

'January 21st. It says here: Tutor on Creative Writing Course Nottingham. Yes, that's right.'

'Just for the record sir; name of people organising it etc. Thank you.' He scribbled something down. 'That's fine. Just to cover us, Sir. I honestly don't think we'll need to trouble you much longer.'

Peter, at this point, more or less caught up with himself, and began to see the irony of the situation. He felt even a little light-headed.

'You seem quite convinced,' he said with a laugh,' that there is no connection between me and your…….quarry?'

'I don't think so. It's profile, you see,' said The Chief Inspector. 'We meet and talk to fraudsters every day, and although we can be fooled now and then, we do get a nose for them. Don't we Sergeant Cork. Sergeant Cork is one of our best profilers.'

Sergeant Cork looked suitably modest. 'Yes it's definitely a …..nose, Sir And you Mr Wood, you'll be delighted to hear, give off quite the wrong scent.'

Peter Wood tried to decide whether he was flattered by this complement.

'And the other thing,' she went on, 'the method you describe in the book of moving money between banks in America, South America and the UK just wouldn't work. The banks sorted that out in the 1990s. So, that puts you into the clear again.'

'The author might have deliberately misled you on that one,' said Peter Wood.

'I doubt it Sir,' said the Chief Inspector. 'I mean, it's alright in a book …you know fiction and all that …but in real life… anyhow, I think that's all. We'll leave you Mr Wood. Thank you for your time and hope we did not interrupt anything you had planned for this evening.'

The sergeant left first. At the door the Chief Inspector paused, and then reached into his pocket to withdraw a second copy of Fool's Gold.

'I wonder Sir, whether you would be so good as to sign this. For my wife. She reads a lot of Crime Fiction. Myself…well I just don't have the …'

'Inclination?'

'That's it. Coals to Newcastle…if you see what I mean.' Peter Wood said that he did, and signed the book with a flourish. He just managed to resist the temptation to write after his name, not guilty.

MR BARNES AND THE SPARROW

The man was standing in the corridor close to the office door. He was like a schoolboy on his first day, uncertain where he should be, yet unwilling to risk asking anyone in case he should be reprimanded, ridiculed or 'shown up'. His clothes ….a tweed jacket, cord trousers, a vaguely regimental tie …reinforced the schoolboy image. Although probably in his forties, the uncertainty in his protruding and watery eyes, together with his uncomfortable stance …he was fiddling with something behind his back ….indicated a kind of childish innocence.

One or two people bustled in and out of the office but he was not able to pluck up courage to ask them where he should be. Neither corridor nor office supplied any clues. His hands moved round in front of him revealing a floppy hat which he tugged at ineffectively as he waited.

A tall uniformed man emerged from the office. 'Oh it's you again, Mr Barnes. Hasn't someone told you where to go?'

Mr Barnes said nothing but hat and eyes shifted even more anxiously, almost as if apologising for inconveniencing anyone, even the friendly Mr Carrick. He followed the officer down the corridor and up the stairs to the third floor and the room where he usually stayed. They knew he liked the room. He stared round its bareness aware that it should be familiar. Putting his bag on the bed he went over to the window. Only when he had looked out was he satisfied that, yes, it was the room he was used to. Carrick left him unpacking his small bag. He spent a long time at the cupboard and the wardrobe arranging his few belongings before he went back to the window again.

Meanwhile downstairs in one of the common rooms, Laski

was helping two other residents to play snooker. He leapt excitedly from one side of the table to the other, peeping under the players' cues, gesticulating, making suggestions and keeping up a non-stop deluge of chatter. It was mostly unfinished sentences, scraps of snooker jargon, combined with tactical advice of a psychological nature. None of this was clear or helpful to the players. Being offered a few seconds before the execution of the stroke, it came too late to be of any value. The player was put off his stroke and, oddly enough, cursed his own lack of skill. There had been an attempt to score; once or twice it had been forgotten, then outrageously miscounted by Laski, then abandoned. The game would soon disintegrate into a row. But Laski's enthusiasm and energy were undiminished.

He was a small ageless man, wiry and bony, who always spoke too quickly, far too quickly to be understood. Words and phrases slid into one another and overlapped like the slapping of waves on a breakwater. He was never at ease, but always full of sly winks to the audience (there was none) and conspiratorial asides to the other player. The same chatter accompanied his visits to the kitchens to 'help out' ….how they dreaded it….or his sallies into the office.

'Can I sharpen these pencils, Mr Carrick?'

'I've just rearranged these files on the shelf here ..is that how you want them?'

Or more irritatingly:

'Wouldn't it be better if supplies came to the kitchen through the side door?'

'Would you like me to rearrange these rotas? Which is more senior Mr Carrick, you or the cook? Because on this list etc etc.'

His sharp eyes, darting glances from beneath comic

eyebrows and one lock of flopped hair, saw into everything and everybody. Yet he never made any lasting impact. He was already moving onto his next encounter, the next involvement, the next interference. The tenuous strand of any relationship that was forged was snapped within a few minutes until the next short-lived strand was spun and thrown aside.

'It's not as if he's actually openly rude,' they said, but he did seem to have the diviner's power of identifying underground streams of malice, pride or complacency in the most well-meaning visitor, sending them away in a confusion or cold rage in five minutes flat.

'Are you here to have a look at us?' he would ask, slipping in one of his malapropisms, or one of his sheer made-up words. 'These people in the common room are the most presentious. I wouldn't go into the kitchen just now …they had an accident with potato peeler, it's like a pig dinner in there. Not the sort of thing decent municipal persons like yourselves want to see. After all it's your hard-earned contrademptions that's gone into the place.'

Most of the officers were thick-skinned enough; they had worse people to deal with. They shrugged and breathed a sigh of relief, at least inwardly, when Laski moved on.

One of Laski's other talents was the ability to trip over furniture, cleaning equipment, himself or others. But without himself coming to any harm. People said that one day he would make some dramatic dive, or give someone an expensive nudge, and then there would be real trouble. But not necessarily for Laski.

Mr Barnes was not much troubled by Laski even though he often shared a room with him. He was hardly aware of people around him; his own anxieties did not allow him to listen to anyone's conversation long, least of all Laski's. While in his room he would rearrange his clothing in the drawers and on the hooks, or stand by the window watching the birds on the telegraph wires or roofs. He would stare at the passing cloud masses, or the tops of the trees in a nearby urban park, or watch the leaves and bits of paper scuttle round in the yard beneath. Then Laski would come bustling in after one of his jaunts round the other rooms, but Mr Barnes was hardly aware of him. And since in any case Mr Barnes had so little to say, Laski usually left him alone.

The hostel itself lay close to the town centre, in an area of early twentieth century housing that had been flattened to accommodate light industry, lock-up units, DIY stores and car parks. Built at the turn of the century, probably as a hospital, it was now a hostel providing food, a bed, occasionally some occupation, and a sort of home, especially during the winter, for homeless men. It was supported by a charity of course but was not the kind of place it was easy to feel charitable about. It was hidden from most people's notice. The people it housed only left or arrived at dawn or dusk, singly, furtively, unnoticed. They hid behind a drabness of dress and an unobtrusive way of walking. None of them were 'filthy old tramps' with cartoon overcoats tied up with string and bottles hidden away in their folds. Some of them, like Mr Barnes, were smart in a genteel but eccentric way. But even with these you could not avoid noticing, as they passed, that faintly musty institutional smell. They went about their everyday lives, slipping in and out of the hostel, and in and out of the town too, never allowing any degree of permanence to stamp them.

From the third floor window Mr Barnes had a good view of that area of the town, but also of the roofs and gutters and down-pipes of the adjacent kitchen wing. This had been added by someone only twenty years ago, and the roof of its two storeys lay just below and to the left of the third floor windows. The addition of the wing had led to a doubling of down-pipes, while some pieces of guttering were stranded, suspended here and there with no apparent function. There were gaps between the slates and the gutters too. The whole area was a trap for blown waste but also a magnificent playground for small birds. Especially the sparrows who could slip in and out of the openings and under the loose slates, reappearing several metres away. Mr Barnes had even observed sparrows taking bits of material into the crevices and he liked to imagine them tucking themselves in somewhere under the roof, cosy and warm, busily maintaining their accommodation and even their personal appearance. Such thoughts drove Mr Barnes back to his own drawers and wardrobe to check and rearrange things. He stood in front of the yellowing mirror, checking his own appearance, straightening his tie, brushing a speck from his jacket. There was no vanity in this, only an anxiety that things should not be allowed to become untidy or get out of control.

The only time that Mr Barnes showed any awareness of a world outside the one he shared with these rooftop birds, was when he went down to watch the wildlife programmes on the television. He seemed to know when these were on as well as he knew the mealtimes. In fact he often had to hurry away from a meal to sit absorbed as some survival scene in the African Rain Forest, or the Kalahari wastes, or the Siberian taiga, or even a Surrey back garden, was enacted. His face showed concentration and traces of other emotions. Young animals, nursing mothers, and small delicate creatures would bring tears to his eyes. Animals at play made him smile faintly. Acts of savagery and aggression …the pursuit and killing of an antelope by a lioness ….upset him so that he trembled. Courtship and mating displays perplexed him. At the end of the programme he returned to his third floor room and watched the passing clouds, the distant tree tops. If he was lucky there would be a lone seagull, some pigeons. And there were always his favourites, the sparrows.

Laski sometimes joined him at the window. Hardly anyone realised it, but these moments were perhaps the only ones of real repose for Laski, apart from when he was actually asleep. He would stand there, making an occasional remark, titbits of advice for the birds. Since Mr Barnes gave no sign of having heard these, Laski learnt to expect no response and lapsed into a brief but almost spell-bound silence.

It was on one of these occasions, the two standing side by side, observant each in his own way, that a sparrow became trapped under a loose piece of wire mesh on a stretch of redundant guttering. The bird had wriggled its way under the mesh, then dislodged part of it so that it slipped over the end of the gutter, trapping the struggling bird. Both Laski and Mr Barnes recognised, early on, a crisis.

'Come on, little bird, this way,' Laski shouted, gesturing wildly.

Mr Barnes remained transfixed, his mouth open.

'There, just a bit behind you. That's right. No, over there, by the slate. Yes, the slate!' Laski continued like a member of the audience shouting encouragement at a game show. Eventually Mr Barnes joined in, clutching at scraps of advice offered by

Laski and repeating them in pitying and almost inaudible fragments.

Eventually Laski broke from the room and went off downstairs jabbering incomprehensibly to anyone he met on his descent. Some tried to make sense of it, others ignored him as they had always done. Not that this deterred Laski. He rushed into the main office, waving wildly, signalling a major emergency.

'Come and look on the roof. It's a sparrow. Trapped! It can't get out.' He shouted knocking over half a dozen files and nearly sprawling on top of them himself.

'Now then, Laski, calm down,' said the Senior Officer. 'I'm just in the middle of a telephone call here. Then I've this laundry list to sort out. I can't be having this stuff about...what did you say? Birds?'

'Someone's got to rescue it!'

'Look here Laski. I'm responsible for a hostel here you know not an aviary or a play-group.'

'But you have to come this minute. It's life or death Mr Steer,' Laski jabbered.'We need ladders, long poles and nets....'

'Do we Laski? Perhaps I ought to call for the fire brigade?'

'Yes Mr Steer. That's it. Can I set off the alarm?'

'Whatever you do, don't touch that alarm! Don't touch anything.'

'But it's urgent Mr Steer.'

'Look, Mr Carrick's in the common room. Ask him to sort things out, okay.' And so Laski shot off in search of that officer.

Meanwhile Mr Barnes was left watching the sparrow's nervous struggles. He slid the window open to get a better view and saw now where the mesh had become entangled with the end of the gutter. His eyes filled with tears. Looking down he saw people passing, and called out feebly:

'Excuse me, I'm sorry but there's a little bird trapped up here, I wonder if you would be so good as to….' But his voice was lost in the wind and the traffic. In any case Mr Barnes was always careful about raising his voice unnecessarily. Taking out a large white handkerchief he wiped the tears from his eyes and then peered along the parapet of stonework that lay just below his window and led along the corner of the building to the adjacent gutter and the trapped bird. The parapet was worn, in urgent need of pointing, and about nine inches wide. He took off his jacket and placed it on a hook in the wardrobe.

Ten minutes later Laski burst into the room followed by Mr Carrick. He had agreed to come with him when he heard that Mr Barnes was upset about the trapped bird. Mr Barnes was seated on the bed, his large clumsy hands clutching the hat. The sparrow was just visible peeping over the brim. Laski leapt to the open window and started to attempt some kind of explanation:

'Mr Barnes has …back to safety…the sparrow,' he mumbled, and then looked back at Mr Barnes, for the first time dumbstruck.

Carrick went over to Mr Barnes and patted him reassuringly on the shoulder. 'Are you alright then, old man?'

Mr Barnes said nothing but just looked down at the sparrow, as if uncertain what should be done with it. Carrick observed the torn trousers, the scuffed shoes; there was brick dust and crumbled stone on his cardigan, even apparently on his cheek and hair. He was trembling, almost swaying as if close to a faint. His short hair was wet with perspiration, and there was a smell of urine.

'Here,' Carrick said. 'let me take it.' Mr Barnes allowed the hat and the sparrow nestling in it to be taken from him.'Best to let it go, eh? I'll take him across to the window, so he can decide.'

'Let it fly away,' were Mr Barnes only words. Once on the window ledge the sparrow flicked away. Mr Carrick stayed at the window, his eyes following the route that Mr Barnes may have taken.

'Was the bird in the gutters above the kitchen,' he asked Laski.

'He was and Mr Barnes, trapped and Mr Barnes ....' But Laski stopped there, not knowing what to say.

Carrick shook his head, eased the window down and came back from the window. Mr Barnes was now beginning to snivel, mumbling explanations and apologies for his' disgraceful state', and that he had 'been to the toilet, Mr Carrick.....in my trousers.'

'Come on Mr Barnes. Let's get you downstairs and sorted out. We'll getyou bath I think, and a change of clothes.'

Eventually Laski told everyone of course and when it had been reluctantly confirmed by Carrick, Mr Barnes found himself something of a local hero. Everyone in the hostel had liked Mr Barnes ...the officers, the residents, even the most casual helpers...and they were all full of admiration and praise. They even seemed to feel a sort of shared pride that one of their number could have shown such courage and compassion.

However a few days' later the mood at the meeting in the main office was less up-beat. There were officials from within and outside the institution; a medical officer, a psychiatric social worker, and several other officials including of course the Senior Officer. Carrick was invited to attend ...but only in a listening capacity.

'I feel that in the interest of this institution....and of course of Mr Barnes,' said the Senior Officer once a report on the incident had been read, 'some more appropriate accommodation for Mr Barnes be sought. He cannot have been fully aware of the dangers he placed himself …and the staff …in by his actions during the 'escapade' No doubt some childish….whim, or hypersensitivity to the plight of the bird must have numbed his mind….the whole rescue operation undertaken in a kind of trance. The trouble is, the man may unwittingly endanger himself again, and put others at risk. This cannot be allowed to happen. My officers are already under considerable stress working here and cannot be expected…'

At this point Carrick, who had told himself that he must not utter a word, broke in angrily.

'Mr Steer, I know I'm probably speaking out of turn….'

'I was going to give you an opportunity to comment Mr Carrick in due course. I suppose you better go ahead now.'

'The way I see it,' said Mr Carrick, 'all this talk of 'trances' is rubbish. You only have to look out of that window and think what was in Mr Barnes mind. He sees the trapped bird. He looks out and inspects the parapet, the gutters, the yard below, and works out a plan. I know a child's plan, but not a sleep-walking one. A plan that's thought through. He takes his jacket off, gets out of the window, before crouching down and shuffling along the parapet, keeping his face against the brickwork, not looking down. Remember, he's big man and not well coordinated. Reaching out he pulls back the mesh, using both hands mind you, and secures the sparrow.'

'Probably put it in his pocket,' suggested someone.

'No, ladies and gentlemen, *inside his hat* which he had remembered to bring with him! Then tucked it all inside his cardigan.'

Surprised grunts greeted these details of Carrick's story 'And then the journey back. I found him eventually sitting on his bed, in a right state, I can tell you, and upset, very upset, but he knew where he was and how he'd got there. He was in shock, who wouldn't be, but he knew what he'd done alright. If he hadn't he'd be a dead man now.'

Carrick sat down to a murmur of sympathy. The Senior Officer now spoke.

'I'd be the last person to suggest that the rescue that Mr Barnes effected wasn't, for someone like Mr Barnes, a plucky one. But still I feel that we have to consider ….Mr Barnes own good …..the protection of the other inmates….that is, the residents…and of course the staff. We have a duty of care and responsibility to…..' He struggled to complete what he had to say.

But the words were not needed. At that moment the outer door of the office was thrust open and Laski plunged in. He tripped on the edge of the carpet and sprawled across the tables where the committee sat, knocking coffee cups and biscuits to the floor. They scrunched under foot, but Laski scorned such irrelevancies. His ear pressed to the door he had heard some of what had been said within.

'Mr Senior Officer sir, we know what you are trying to do. To get rid of Mr Barnes. His humane rights are being viciously stampled on! You, all of you,'and his upraised finger swung in an accusing arc round the room,' are implicit. You can't wash your feet of this…not in a thousand years.'

The people round the table looked at Laski as if stunned. Carrick and another officer conducted Laski from the room, but he continued to shout with unusual clarity, for the benefit now of the other residents:

'They're going to put our Mr Barnes away, in a nut-house. Incarcify him, just because he did that brave thing. You see, there'll be bars on all the windows, the glass painted black. And the birds,' and this was the last thing they heard,' will all be gunned down, slaughtered, no mercy. A hypocaust.'

It was eventually agreed at the meeting that there would be no change of policy. The Psychiatric Social worker would interview Mr Barnes and Mr Carrick was charged with keeping a special eye on him. Someone suggested that Mr Barnes be moved to the ground floor, but Mr Carrick was able to point out that such a mildly precautionary measure would hit Mr Barnes very hard. He promised he would have a talk with Mr Barnes. He might even discreetly secure the lower section of the sash window.

Someone raised the question of Laski's behaviour and strangely enough most people were more amused by the incident than disturbed by it. It was felt that he could be 'contained' and was no real danger to anyone. The meeting broke up with the feeling that they had sorted things pretty well.

The relationship between Laski and Mr Barnes was never quite the same again. Once Laski had been pacified and assured that the Mr Barnes was not going to be moved, he began to adopt the position of protector, and to some extent, promoter of Mr Barnes as some kind of circus freak or trapeze artist. Laski's frequent recounting of the incident embarrassed Mr Barnes. In fact, on one occasion it was Laski himself who was restrained by Mr Barnes's mildly reproving:

'I say Laski, you do exaggerate things a bit. Don't you think you could go and help them in the kitchen?'

And Laski went off, happily obedient, even glorying in his obedience to the instructions from his heroic room mate.

CHESTER

‘Have you met Chester yet?’

‘Who’s Chester when he’s at home?’

‘Come on, John. He’s been here for two weeks now. Arrived during your trip to South America. Come and see for yourself.’

John Protheroe is drinking coffee with Fenella in the canteen at the Animal Rehab Centre where they are assistants. Both of them are concerned with the health and rehabilitation of exotic animals …she with mammals, he with reptiles. The animals come to the centre either from zoos that have closed down or from unsuitable domestic environments. Most of their charges have been subject to stress and need both medical attention and psychological help. Snakes and lizards for instance; kept as pets in some overheated semi, competing with cats, dogs and small children for space tend to become very uptight about it all. Once the centre has sorted them out, snakes or monkeys or parrots, whatever, it endeavours to return the creatures to appropriate zoos and sanctuaries.

Both John Protheroe and Fenella work in their respective sections without regular assistants. She is five years younger than him, very pretty, always full of enthusiasm in an unaffected way. John is more morose …perhaps in keeping with the creatures he tends…and doesn’t wear his heart on his sleeve. Fenella likes to share the problems and triumphs of her work. John is a listening ear, and sometimes a shoulder to cry on, roles that he admits he finds quite enjoyable. For Fenella takes her work very seriously. Hence she takes John less seriously.

‘So which is Chester?’ he says, glancing round at the cages of assorted animals, many of which…or is it many of whom?...are staring at him with varying degrees of curiosity or hostility.

'Over here,' she says, pointing to her desk. Seated at the computer keyboard, a slightly puzzled smirk on its ancient face, is a young chimpanzee. In one hand he holds a pencil, in the other an unpeeled orange.

'Come over here, Ches dear, and say hello to John.' Shyness overcomes Chester and he tries to hide under the desk. Fenella coaxes him out but he still clings tightly to her as she carries him across to John. He is allowed to curl a finger round Chester's finger tips, but the chimpanzee is unwilling to look him in the eye. Apparently he was brought into a local port by some eccentric sea-captain. The vessel, m.v. Chester, had been declared unseaworthy, the crew had vanished, and the captain was holed up in some hostel. Two weeks later the chimp was discovered, left on board, and suffering from severe malnutrition and an influenza-like complaint.

'But we soon put you back on the right road, didn't we Ches, my love,' says Fenella.

'Very lucky to survive I should think. Influenza can be a killer…'

'Shush, John. No so loud,' she says clutching Chester more closely. 'Don't want to scare him.'

'Don't be silly, Fenella…he can't understand.'

'Perhaps not ….but we don't know do we? Not for sure. Actually John I've been doing a bit of reading. It's amazing what they can learn. Especially when they have someone to bond with, someone to relate to. They become more receptive. They can be taught things. Not just tricks. They really learn and understand.'

'I'm sure you're right. But our job is rehabilitation, Fenella. Get them healthy, get them adjusted. Pass them on to the proper people.'

'Absolutely. But Chester isn't ready for that yet. See how upset he was when you came in. Long way to go yet. He's still seriously underweight, aren't you my pet?' she says pressing her hand to his stomach. An expression which John could only call coy flickers across Chester's face. And a little kernel of resentment stirs in John's own stomach.

Over the next few weeks Chester, according to Fenella, makes a slow recovery from his ailments, but even more rapid educational advances. At coffee breaks John finds her pre-occupied. On one day Chester has a relapse and she tells John that she had to stay up with him all night.

'You look done in. Look why don't you go and have a nap for a couple of hours while I sit by his sick bed.'

'So kind of you, John.'

'We don't want to see you getting ill…'

She looks at him puzzled for a moment, and then laughs. 'Oh silly me. I meant kind to poor old Chester.'

John spends the next couple of hours trying to communicate with Chester but either because of his illness, or Fenella's absence, it doesn't seem to work. He stares at John truculently, refuses all playthings and makes a pretence of sleeping. When Fenella returns however Chester is suddenly wide awake. She gathers him into her arms and they embrace fiercely. With a sigh John went back to his reptiles.

After Chester's recovery Fenella becomes involved in lengthy exercise sessions with him. 'He's working things out …in that little head of his,' she reports gleefully. She describes an experiment she is conducting: bunch of bananas suspended from the ceiling of the high cage, boxes and sticks placed on one side, he has to assemble them and climb up and get at the fruit with the stick.

'Textbook stuff!' John says. 'We did all that at college.' Fenella is not listening. 'Do you know what he first did when I left him in the cage?'

'Tried to jump?'

'That's right. But…'

'It was far too high.'

'Of course. Do you know what he did then, the rascal?'

'Ran over to the computer and started to work out a programme for his options?'

'Now be serious, John.'

'All right then. He picked up a stick and started whacking the bars of the cage.'

'That's exactly what he did,' crestfallen. 'How did you know?'

'I told you Fenella. I've read all the articles.'

She looks disappointed. 'Anyhow, I've got him to start investigating the boxes. It won't be long before…'

'Be sure to time him,' he says, not altogether seriously.

Three days later when she does manage to snatch a few seconds for a visit to the canteen, she joins John.

'Bananas reached. Textbook route. Three minutes thirty seconds. By next week he'll be doing it in two minutes. Isn't he a clever little fellow?'

'Of course he is, 'he says. No point in upsetting her. It seems a good moment to try another tack. 'Why not come out to dinner with me to celebrate? We could talk about old Chester there at leisure. I know a nice little Italian place.'

'Good of you to show an interest, John. But I've got so much to do. I'll be working late.'

'On your own, of course.'

'Not at all. There'll be Chester.'

'How silly of me to forget,' he says, not hiding his cynicism. But she is oblivious.

'Even if someone were to break in, a burglar say, I'm sure Chester would rally to my defence,' she says with a grin.

'You mean he'd throw his stick and bananas at him?'

'No seriously, I think he's very protective.'

Gradually John's mood becomes blacker. He imagines Fenella and Chester locked in close embrace, cooing into each others ears like wood-pigeons. Slim fingers clutch knotted ones, head is pressed close to her chest. And those eyes, knowing. Confident, adoring.

A few days' later Fenella comes dashing into the reptile section. 'Come straight away,' she shouts, completely ignoring the stressed-out python John is cleaning up. 'Be first to see what Chester has done!'

Chester is seated at the desk. The cage door is open, the bananas suspended, accessible as per textbook. Boxes in a neat pile. Stick placed neatly on top.

'So,' he says, sarcasm hardly disguised. 'What's he done now? Broken the world record or something?'

'No Donald. I just want you to examine the situation. With your scientific hat on. I've got it on video anyhow, but I just need you to confirm things…'

'Confirm what?'

'That he's done what he has.'

'Done what? Things look perfectly normal to me.'

'Exactly John. That's just the point. I didn't set this up for him. The boxes were over there in the cupboard, the bananas were on the shelf, with the stick. Do you see what he's done. He's set the whole experiment up himself, while I was out of the room. Don't you see? It's his way of saying, come on, it's all only an exercise. Give me something that demands real intelligence!' He looks across at Chester. And this time there is no doubt, the smirk of complacency in those close-set eyes. There is too no denying the adoration in Fenella's face as she goes over to Chester and bestows a kiss on his wrinkled forehead.

'Brilliant,' he says, seething with conflicting emotions. But there is no doubt in his mind which is the dominant one.

John knows now that it is time for him to take up the challenge seriously. Back at his desk he retrieves the letter he remembers receiving from the Californian Institute for Primate Research. He hadn't realised its value at the time. The institute are seeking suitable apes for an extensive programme of investigations into animal intelligence. Especially chimpanzees for their brand new lateral thinking programme. He finds the web site and sends off a message, giving the name of their head of centre (who is fortunately away in darkest Africa and more or less out of contact) and his chief assistant for primates, Miss Fenella Cooper. He mentions the 'precocious gifts of one particular chimpanzee.' He doesn't feel very ashamed; after all he isn't telling any lies.

A week or so later Fenella, a perplexed look on her brow, shows him a letter she's just received. He reads it, pretending to be mystified by the Californian letterhead. It is an invitation for Fenella to send details of Chester's performance etc if possible on video.

'Well I suppose it might be some kind of…opportunity for

Chester,' he says guardedly. 'A pity that he isn't really suitable.'

'Why not?'

'His recuperation…you know …not being quite complete. In any case I know how closely attached you two are.' Fenella looks at John doubtfully. 'Actually he's much better now, and as for the two of us getting on well, that's no reason for me to stand in his way.'

'Just thinking what would be best for Chester.'

'That's very thoughtful of you John. But whatever you say, I think he should go to California, to be with the other apes on this programme. Not just messing about here with us.'

'You've done wonders with him Fenella.' Magnanimity ascendant, jubilance hopefully veiled.

'Maybe,' says Fenella. 'But I'm still going to e mail them now. After all, it will be the right thing for Chester, won't it.'

'You may be right, Fenella.'

And that is that. Several weeks later Chester is shipped off. Fenella is tearful, while he can barely contain his good fortune. And the smirk on Chester's face as they install him in his air-freight cage has gone. He just looks perplexed, poor fellow, thinks John. Still, he'll soon have something to get his lateral grey cells working on. Without Fenella's encouragement.

A week later John is talking to Fenella again in the canteen. It's like old times. She seems to be getting over parting with Chester very stoically, he thinks.

'You know, I think Chester's going was a good thing for me,' she says. 'I was getting too attached.'

'You were certainly very…close,' he says sympathetically. 'You encouraged him, and he responded. As any creature would you befriended.'

'Actually,' she says, head on one side, 'it was probably a good thing for you too John?'

'How do you mean?' he says, trying not to sound hopeful.

'Well I think Chester was beginning to get a teeny-weeny bit jealous of you. He was only a child after all, you know, emotionally. I think he found relationships between grown-ups …all our fairly organised and mature emotional responses ….. …rather baffling.'

John looks down at the table hiding his glowing cheeks and neck.

'In any case,' she goes on. 'It means I can concentrate my attentions elsewhere.' She gets up from the table. 'Now, why don't you come and have a look at …. Desmond. He's a real cutie!'

John followed her wearily back to the primate section.

BRANDENBURG IN THE FIFTIES

Unusual experiences and their locations don't necessarily match up. Take this gymnasium for instance. Not really the place you'd choose for a musical revelation. The ropes coiled up near the ceiling, the wall-bars, the mottled yellow floor timber, the piles of mats and strange humped bits of equipment. At one end there are stacks of plastic chairs because this gym is used for all sorts of purposes. This particular night it is our evening orchestra practice under our conductor, Mr Garnett. About a dozen adults and several teenagers like me, invited because we are Mr Garnett's pupils. We are playing the usual classical repertoire for such a group, although I'm too much of a novice to realise that.

In order to conduct Mr Garnett sits at the front on a school desk. There's nothing stylish about his conducting. In fact he hardly ever gets to his feet and his hands give only minimal gestures. He smokes continuously. Even when I have my individual lesson at his home, I never see him without a cigarette, even when he is playing the violin himself. I watch entranced as the curl of ash lengthens and eventually cascades down into the f holes of the violin. For Mr Garnett ash trays are redundant.

This particular evening we play some familiar items: Mozart, Haydn, Percy Grainger. They are string arrangements of suites and symphonies. I enjoy the playing, the music-making, but only in a fairly unfocused uncommitted way. This is a better way of spending an evening than sitting at home doing homework. I have no special favourites and no great confidence or prowess. I sit near the back and play quietly.

Eventually on the is particular evening, Mr Garnett grabs hold of another folder and dishes copies out to us. Brandenburg III it says. 'You lot,' he says to those of us sitting at the back, 'Move over and make space for yourselves. You'll be the third fiddles.' That sounds easy work to me. Then I look at the copy and my heart sinks; it's a riot of black notes!

Mr Garnett gives us the signal to start. And suddenly it is as if I have been enrolled in whatever the equivalent of the present-day Red Arrows would have been in the fifties. Almost everyone hurls themselves into the fray. They've played this before, I think to myself. I sit in my chair, bow poised motionless, hoping I won't be noticed. On all sides the forward momentum and the pulse is so breathtaking that I wonder how anyone can stay with it. Eventually, taking my life in my hands, I plunge in, unbelievably at the right place. And keep going. The effect is more exhilarating than anything I have done before. The dodgems and the big dipper at the Goose Fair are tame compared with this. But in a way it is quite like being on one of those rides…the music is carrying me along. The music is playing me. It's just a question of holding on tight.

At one point the music seems to be constructed from a series of running questions and answers from each section of the orchestra, including the third violins. There is a moment of hesitation around me, and Mr Garnett shouts out: 'Thirds! Here's you entry. Now!' Bang! We all bomb in, unbelievably again at the right place, sucked along by the glorious surge of sounds on all sides. Then we suddenly seem to fan out, scattering to right and left, up and down, as if we were indeed those fighter aircraft performing a looping manoeuvre, high above the clouds. We skim into open sky, and then are brought back again, the circle completed, and power along, wing-tip to wing-tip, twenty feet above the ground. I think I am holding my breath, and in danger of passing out, but somehow my bow and fingers keep going.

And then it's all over. Several seconds of silence, slumped in our chairs, my heart pounding. And then the audible exhalation of breath and someone lets out a whoop, two people are laughing slightly hysterically, other grinning and exchanging wry comments. Even the most serious ones, the old hands, can't hide their smirks. Mr Garnett rubs his hands together and I notice that, for the first time, that he has put his cigarette down on the desk where it is smouldering close to the edge.

I just sit there. I have crossed some kind of musical Rubicon. Broken my own sound barrier. And I suspect there is never going to be any going back.

UP IN SMOKE

I caught sight of it by chance; a delicately-carved wooden music-stand just visible over people's shoulders. It was off the main square, beyond the crowds. I negotiated my way past piles of bric-a-brac, a stuffed fox in a glass case, a jumble of pottery in boxes, and piles of paperback books. There were several trestle tables, but not very much to show except for three or four violins nestling in lush violet-coloured felt, a clarinet on a stand and a trumpet. Then I could see the music stand quite clearly & was able to get close enough to inspect it. It was not in as good condition as I had hoped. The arched legs were no longer really symmetrical, and there were suspicious glints of glue along some of the joints.

In any case did I really have any use for another music-stand? In its favour, one could say that it was decorative, the carving wasn't too crude, the yellowish wood looked as if it would clean up. But in terms of a functioning music stand it really wouldn't do; almost any cheap metal one would be as serviceable. After all, I wasn't in a position to buy anything. I had just wandered out of the hotel, after breakfast, intending to walk along the avenue that topped the low encircling city walls. There were the usual cyclists, a couple of caribinieri on horseback, the hazy view across to the Apuan Alps. But at one of the gates I had suddenly looked back into town and seen the stalls, and remembered that today there would be an antique fair in the city's main square and adjacent side-streets.

I hadn't a penny in my pocket so even if the stand had been more promising ….?

I was going to turn away when my eye was caught by the

woman at one end of the trestles. She had her back to me and was busy on a mobile phone. I wondered at the confusion of long dark hair, slim hand holding the phone, and thought, well I could just ask for the price of the stand. Then she turned round and caught sight of me. Hurriedly she completed the call, and came over.

'I'm sorry,' she said, in English, 'but I was speaking to my family.'

'It's okay,' I said, 'I wasn't in a hurry. I was wondering about the price. It says something here, but I can't make it out.'

'Oh dear, that is an old price. Yes…four hundred thousand lire.' She looked at me anxiously. 'That does seem quite expensive.'

'Considering its condition….' I began to say. I didn't want to offend. In any case I couldn't work out what that many lire might be in euros.

'Perhaps you would like to offer something. I think the stand is not in very good condition. What about one hundred and fifty euros?' I looked again at the dark rather mournful eyes and wondered whether the hint of sadness was being put on. The rest ofthe stuff on the tables didn't look very attractive, and she certainly wasn't doing much business. Was she expecting me to buy out of pity?

'What about a hundred euros?' I said with a shrug. And I really didn't want the stand.

There was a short pause while she considered. My heart sank; I really had no idea about this bargaining business.

'Let me ask my colleague,' she said eventually, and walked away to speak on the mobile phone again. She seemed to be waiting for someone to be brought to the phone at the other end, but she smiled prettily in my direction. It was slightly embarrassing just standing there, looking at her, so I turned my attention to the violins. As far as I could tell they were ordinary factory-made instruments, but set up with reasonable strings and the bows were probably sound. There were several boxes of books, all in Italian, cheap novels I supposed, together with some children's books. At the bottom of one box there was a folder. When I opened it up I could see that it contained sheet music … violin and piano pieces. Pot-boilers, like the Meditation from Thais, Brahms Hungarian Dances. As I drew them out of the cardboard box, the folder's cover, which appeared to be made up of several sheets of thick paper bound together, tore on a staple in the side of the box. On the inside of the cover I caught sight of a manuscript, hand-written, on creamy grey paper, a lot of flourishes, and a title: Concerto a tre.

Pulling back the paper I peered inside the cover. And was I imagining it, but there seemed to be an almost imperceptible rise in temperature. A prickly feeling in my hands and wrists, as if I were holding something that had been suppressed, even imprisoned, and was being brought out into the open.

On the other hand it may have been something to do with the warm sunshine, the crowds, and the woman on the phone. I managed to pull back some more of the torn cover, to ascertain that there were two staves of music, but three parts and a figured bass underneath the bottom one. Another tug revealed the initials H.P. and then some words in flowing script: … 'a just imitation of the fam'd Italian masters…' Strange. The words rang a bell. But then the woman returned and I only half listened while she told me the price for the stand. I hardly heard her because a more insistent debate was going on inside my head.

Surely this wasn't just about instincts, prickly feelings. Had not my time, at long last, come? On the other hand, perhaps I should have been dismissing the whole business at the outset.

I remembered as a kid going fishing on the canal. Hoping for a great catch. And everybody watching. But of course then when it did surface; thank goodness, no one was looking. All eyes on their own lines. Because the size of the tiddler I'd caught wasn't going to turn any heads.

And one part of me said, okay, that was fishing. You were only a kid then. And you never did strike it lucky. Not as far as you can remember. So why should you be lucky now, here, thirty years later in this market place in sunny Italy. After all this time. A relatively unblemished, mostly sensible and safe life. A music librarian. Looking after music, hoarding it, treasuring it so to speak, supplying orchestras and choral groups with sets of this and that. A reputation for being reliable, even diligent in searching the catalogues. But a man for the stuff of life-changing encounters? No. Revelations and discoveries? Not me. Unless this was the big one and it had my name on it. Not that I was purely a desk man. Well, not that kind of desk. Weekly I struggled to hold my own in the back desks of the second violin section in a local string orchestra. And most of my spare time was spent listening to music, reading about music. My head full of quotes and snippets of information. But the dream of doing some real research, revealing something completely new and exciting about some half-forgotten composer, remained a dream.

But now here it was. At long last. The classic story book situation: the Right person in the Right place at the Right time! Wasn't that how it was supposed to happen? Forget about your gawky adolescent angler hopeful but hopeless on the canal bank. Think Music Librarian, warm Italian market, pretty dark-haired girl in the background. Might not I have some kind of special affinity with this kind of place and situation. Instincts and calling both told me that what was unfolding in this market square might be my longed-for moment of truth. Surely the feeling in my fingers when I'd first pulled back the cover confirmed that. I looked down. No ordinary fingers those .. half a lifetime teasing out and caressing documents, books, maps, charts and papers. And stamping them with a return date too I suppose. But fingers surely that were specially attuned, ultra-sensitive! And wasn't it also especially auspicious that I had also a musical ear, one that could catch the arch of melody, the sad cadence, the nonchalant stroll of the bass. Even if I wasn't very proficient at actually delivering any of those things.

Above all there was of course those initials, HP, surely Henry Purcell Who else could it be? I ran through some other composers with a capital P, but no one came up with a Christian name starting with an aitch Maybe Heinrich, Harold, or even Hermione? No it had to be a Henry. And so, a Concerto by Purcell. Why not? But I seemed to remember that he wrote no concertos. On the other hand, Corelli did and about at the same Time. But not Henry. But who says he didn't! How sure were they? Those words on the manuscript: 'in homage to the Italians masters'?. Surely, here in this antique market in central Italy the extraordinary discovery could be made. Henry Purcell having a stab at what the Italians did by the hundreds. And discovered by me.

The girl was looking at me. Expectant. Had she named a price for the stand? I gaped. The dark eyes looked at me, amused. Then she scribbled a figure onto a slip of paper. It was quite reasonable. But of course I didn't want it.

'If you don't mind, I'll think about it…'

She looked crestfallen. I grabbed hold of the folder, trying to hide the tear. 'But I'll take these.'

She leafed through the folder cover, shook her head at the tear, and found a price. Just a few euros. I reached in my pocket. I hadn't brought any loose change. Fortunately I had a credit card in my wallet, but she shook her head. Ridiculous in any case. For just a few euros?

'Look, I'll get some cash,' I said. 'I'll be back here in no time. Keep these for me.'

She placed the folder on a small table behind her. 'They'll be here for you.' Another intimate smile.

I don't know why but it seemed to be important that I get the money as soon as possible. I rushed out of the side street into the market place, looking round desperately for a bank or a cash machine. Of course I knew that the whole thing might be a mistake. I was in no position to know whether it was genuine, to authenticate it. I would have to get it back to England, take it to real experts, the Bodleian, the British Library. It could just turn out to be some student exercise, or some valueless fake given a spurious Purcellian background to make it saleable. Completely unconvincing except to a fool.

But at the same time it might also be the real thing. Purcell's so far unrecorded experiment into baroque music in the real Italian style. And whose hands better than mine to convey this discovery to the desks and the admiring eyes of those who could indeed authenticate it.

Eventually I found a machine, but had to wait in a long

queue of tourists. As I stood there fuming, it suddenly came to me that the woman with the long dark hair, might try to remedy the tear, look again at what the tear was revealing, and realize that it was the hidden manuscript in the cover that I was after, not the contents. And come to the conclusion that it was something special. The price tag of a few euros might suddenly rocket.

At the machine, a moment of sheer panic: my pin number completely evaded me. Fumbling in my wallet, I managed to find the scrap of paper on which I had recorded it, in code. But how did you work it out? More dithering and delay. But if I gave the wrong pin number my card might be gobbled up. Behind me in the queue, a large woman in a huge sun hat, was beginning to look anxious.

By a supreme effort of will I closed my eyes, flushed all thoughts from my head and got the pin number right, and punched it in. I felt almost sick with relief when the notes came slipping out. I turned to rush off back up to the market. There was a touch on my shoulder. It was the woman in the sun hat, an expression of pity on her face. She proffered the card I had left in the machine. Thanking her I rushed away.

When I got back to the square nothing seemed to have changed. The girl was talking to a couple with a ten year-old son who were inspecting a clarinet in a case. It was clear that they were only casually interested. I looked for the folder. It was not on the table where she had placed it. But that didn't make me panic. There were so many piles of items here and there, I couldn't be sure quite where she had placed it.

Then the family moved away. She came to me, smiling. "Ah you come back.' As if I might not! I was tempted to reach across and kiss those smiling lips. I promised myself that when my ship came in, properly, when my name was officially pronounced and celebrated as the discoverer of the lost Purcell manuscript, that I would return and share the rewards, whatever they might be, with her. For ever.

She was handing an almost brand new slim box file to me. I opened it, and yes, inside was the sheet music.

'But the cover,' I said. My throat dry.

'Oh that. I threw it away. It was awful.'

'But…' I looked round me, at the floor, expecting any moment to see the torn paper, the 'Concerto a tre' flapping, or scrunched under the feet of the crowd.

'Away?' I said foolishly.

She smiled again winningly, gesturing to a brazier that was smouldering behind the stall and from which a column of grey smoke was issuing. And for a few seconds I heard and probably smelt too the faint but final strains of some baroque English masterpiece disappearing into the unforgiving Italian sky.

AFRICAN CARVING

The carved figure stood on the lid of the piano. It was about twelve inches tall in light brown unvarnished wood. It was always there when he had his lesson. Miss Goltz sometimes edged it back from the keyboard, but it was never removed. Throughout their playing it stood there, mute, apparently unlistening, even though it was in fact a musician.

He had decided to take piano lessons again. He had been a competent pianist, but had let things slip a bit. Miss Margaret Goltz was recommended…a teacher of the old school and very particular but he didn't mind that. But even he was surprised at the time they spent on scales and simple melodic exercises. They had to be played in two ways. First: with all the notes equally weighted. She stopped him frequently after two or three notes:

'Mr Allen. You are not listening. They must be absolutely even. The G A B C…no variation.' And he tried it again until she was grudgingly satisfied.

Then there was the second version. Here the emphasis was on the phrasing of the sequence of notes. It applied of course to both the scales and then the melodies of the sonatas they worked on.

'The group of notes must form a phrase, it must be …. organic,' she explained.

He tried again.

'But the first note Mr Allen. You play it as if it were merely the …first note. It is more than that….the phrase is launched by it….' and she demonstrated.

Then they moved onto middle of the tune, or the phrase,

which was an arching one. He played it, observing hairpins to make it rise and fall.

'Good', she said. 'That is what is needed. The dynamics.' At least I'm getting the hang of something he said to himself. 'But,' and his heart fell. 'You have to feel the phrase as a whole, so that it doesn't merely go up and then go down, but that it is an entity that 'ascends', lingers, and then 'dies away." She illustrated this with a quick swoop of her delicate but wrinkled wrist and fingers.

'So I suppose it's really a question of slowing the notes down here, and quickening them up there,' he said lamely.

'Probably. If we were to measure what we did with scientific instruments. But it is the music that dictates what you do with the phrase, not some rule or procedure.'

He looked at the keyboard and thought: she does wrap it up a bit. Still that's what I'm paying for.

'You probably think I'm fussy about playing scales so evenly in the first place. But it means that you have control of your fingers, and then they can respond precisely and sensitively to the demands of the music.'

'I think I understand,' he said in the end. 'But sometimes I wonder whether it's just better to get on and play …and let things work themselves out.'

'Sometimes yes, Mr Allen. Of course you must have that freedom. But you don't need me to coach you in that freedom.'

'Don't get me wrong Miss Goltz. What you are doing is transforming my playing.'

He saw her eyebrows tighten slightly, and there was the ghost of a smile on her lips. Was she pleased with his compliment, or quietly amused by it?

Later over coffee she asked him about his chamber music playing.

'Oh it's just with a friend of mine. He plays the clarinet and his wife plays the viola. We have a bash at Mozart, Brahms that sort of thing.'

'Ah Mozart of course …you mean the K 498. The Kegelstatt.'

'Yes we call it the 'skittle alley trio'. You can just see it can't you, old Mozart…you know with that flourishing thing, at the start, like someone sending a ball belting down the alley or wherever it was.'

'Yes, that gesture, or flourish. But then the delicacy of it … …like a well-executed bow.' She looked fleetingly at the carved figure on the piano and moved it slightly forward. Then she said: 'Apparently they say the skittle alley, or bowling alley, connection is pretty dubious.'

'Pity.'

'I agree. If it helps us to play the music with that spirit, why not"

Then she said with what appeared to be hesitation: 'You must bring the music along one day. We could have a look at it.'

'I've got it here,' he said, reaching for his bag.

She studied the first page of the music, noting the edition and some pencil notes in the margin.

'Why not just play this first page,' she said. 'Don't worry. I'm not going to put you off with stops and starts, or analyzing it.'

Cautiously, and with a little hesitation he began. 'Flourish', he thought, 'oh dear, more like someone falling over!' But after a while he got into his stride. Then at the point where the clarinet entered and he was accompanying, she suddenly began to sing the part quietly. The low contralto pitch of her voice and the quiet unhesitating tone surprised him. He had not expected ....

'Your voice, Margaret. Lovely. Contralto. I hadn't expected it. You should sing more often.'

She had been playing the slow movement on the piano and singing, well really humming the viola part. Morris had not yet turned up. Ade was cleaning his clarinet but stopped to listen before delivering this compliment.

She pressed harder into the playing to cover her embarrassment. As a third year student at the Royal College she was specialising in accompaniment, and was encouraged to take any opportunities that arose. She had played chamber music with Morris the viola player on several occasions. It was he who had invited the Nigerian medical student Adetunde to come and play trios: Mozart, Brahms, and Bartok.

She would have hesitated to say it to anyone but she knew that they fell in love through the Mozart. It was not just that compliment about her voice. Right from the start they had felt an intimacy in the way piano and clarinet parts interwove, questioning and answering, as if in a game or a drama. Of course Morris played his part and he was no mean musician. But with and between Margaret and Ade it was different. Ade courted her for several weeks, took her out for meals, bought her flowers, and they continued to meet even when the trio rehearsals were over. At times especially in the presence of other people she was acutely aware of the differences between them. But not the colour or racial difference.

'When I first met you,' said Ade one day, 'I thought you were very severe. Very reserved. If you don't like a thing, your lips tense, just a little, your eyebrows are raised by just a millimetre. I thought at first how English.'

'Actually it's the Eastern European in me. My grandparents came here from Germany just before the first world war.' Looking at Ade she thought, yes what a difference. She was constantly astounded at the range of expressions that played on his face, delight, exaggerated horror, laughter, acute disappointment, all danced across his smiles and frowns like some ballet. He was always on the move, always in a rush, yet enjoying what he was doing so hugely that it was infectious. Margaret found herself bubbling, even fooling about, 'dancing in the streets' she called it. And Ade in his turn now found himself following her mood, sitting down and contemplating, wondering, practically philosophising. But when they were playing it was different. It was as if each jumped out of their own skins and inhabited a dual one together in the music. If for both of them the precision of the playing was important, it only served as a spring board for playing the music. She knew that she played better than before when they were together. The seriousness in her and his energy were partners in the flow of the music.

Ade's medical studies kept him very busy, but he still found the time to play chamber music. His clarinet playing was something astonishing. It was as if lungs, diaphragm, mouth, and lips had been designed with the clarinet in mind. Or the other way round. He played jazz occasionally but said that it did not really satisfy him, the way the Mozart or Brahms did. On one occasion he was invited to play the Quintet with a famous quartet. His control of lower register notes, his phrasing, and his lyricism always seemed to inspire others to play even better.

Eventually she and Ade became lovers. They both had tiny bedrooms in shared flats so it was difficult. They discussed finding a shared flat for two, but she noticed that Ade was not enthusiastic about the search.

On one of their Sunday walks through a London park, Ade told her about his parents who lived on the eastern borders of Western Nigeria, an area close to the delta. His dad was something in local government, not well off. Ade was on a government scholarship.

'News from home is very troubling,' he said. 'It doesn't seem to match with what we see in the papers or on the television.'

'Is there a war on, officially?'

'Oh yes, officially and in reality. We in Nigeria always have this problem with unity. You British made it for us, but didn't really look at what you were trying to impose a kind of unity on. So things break down. This Colonel Ojukwu has tried to take the East out of Nigeria and create the new state of Biafra.'

'So do your people in Western Nigeria hate the people in the East?'

'The Yoruba, hate the Ibo? Not really. But then the North is involved too. It is very complicated. And friction and distrust can soon turn into hatred.'

'How far away is the fighting?'

'That's precisely what I can't discover. A hundred miles? Twenty?'

Later she asked him why he chose to study medicine rather than music.

'I never considered music ….it was just there and I did it. Nigeria always needs her doctors.'

She tried to imagine the anxiety of being separated from home and family and the lack of communication. 'My parents live in Shropshire,' she told him. 'Both used to be language teachers, although both are retired they do a bit of teaching in adult education. But I can pop back home anytime, whereas you…'

'But you talked about Eastern Europe.'

'That was my grandparents. We are completely anglicized now, I should think.'

'But there might be a bit of Mozart, in the blood?'

'It's the sort of thing I like sometimes to imagine,' she said with a laugh.

'And you have brothers and sisters?'

'Four. They're all older than me. I came very late.'

'It would be nice to meet them.'

'Yes you should. I was going to say …what about Christmas…?'

'Traditional English Christmas? That would be nice.' She was silent for a while. They were sitting by a lake with ducks. He took her hand, placed it parallel to his own.

'How will your parents feel about all this, you know? The black man and their daughter.'

'Oh I think they'll be fine,' she said with an air of confidence. Well they'd have to be wouldn't they. It wasn't a thing she was anxious about. Their studies kept them apart for most of the day. Margaret had her practising to do at the College since she could only play for a limited time on the rickety piano in the flat. Ade's medical studies were now becoming more time-consuming and he was not able to spend time at the college. Just occasionally they managed to play duets, or trios with Morris. And there were the very occasional returned tickets to public concerts, the

Festival Hall, Wigmore Hall, or one of the City churches, which the college passed on to them.

Only on a Sunday with her flat mates away did they manage to have a day to themselves, staying in bed late, reading Sunday papers, eating chaotic meals, making love whenever they felt like it. One of the other Sundays, when they were feeling fed up, and crowded in by flatmates, Ade said: 'Can't we go somewhere exciting? Just you and me.'

'You mean …the South coast. Like Brighton.'

'No. Not Brighton.'

'Well what about Paris, or Vienna. We could hear some music.'

They looked at some brochures, and he became more excited. Then suddenly, he threw them to one side.

'What's up?' she said.

'Oh nothing. Who needs Paris? Or Vienna?'

'But you said somewhere different. Exciting.'

'Perhaps I don't know what I want.'

'Getting bored…'

'Margaret, Don't. It's just that …..I was looking at the prices. There's no way I could afford that sort of money, even for one. We need to find something more reasonable.'

The brochure had listed only one and two star hotels. Margaret knew that there was nothing more 'reasonable' unless they went for youth hostels. And that wasn't what they wanted. 'The trouble is,' he went on, 'that my money doesn't always arrive. From the Government. And I can't expect my parents to send me much. And with this war on, it could all fall apart.'

'How do you mean?'

'I might just have to go home.'

'Right. Listen to me Ade but don't say anything. I'm well off, really well off compared with you. I want you to take me on holiday to Paris. I've got the money for both of us, just for three or four days. Just some two star place.'

'I couldn't do that Margaret.'

'I thought you loved me…'

'That's exactly why I couldn't…'

'Pride? Can't let a lady pay the bill?'

'Margaret!'

'Look this is just a one off. Like a present. I take you to Paris. I won't do it again. Once you're a brilliant doctor I'll expect you to do half of the paying, if not more.'

'It doesn't seem right.'

'If you really love me, you'll let me do it. With you and me pride doesn't have to come into it.'

'I suppose not' he said doubtfully. They arranged to fly to Paris for a three day stay a month hence.

A week before departure Ade showed Margaret a letter from Nigeria. It said that further payments towards his education could no longer be guaranteed. 'But we are still going to Paris,' she said defiantly. Then, the day before departure, their bags already packed, Ade received an urgent message from Nigeria. The war zone was reported a few miles from his home village. His parents did not demand his return but he read between the lines that they would like him to. 'I have to go back,' he said. 'If I can get a flight.'

'We can go to Paris any time,' she said. 'When you get back.' Two days later he managed to get a flight to Lagos. Margaret went to the airport to see him off. She had never seen Ade so preoccupied, so upset at the way things had developed. Before he went off through the barrier he squeezed her so hard that she gasped. 'I'll be back,' he said. 'As soon as I can.'

Margaret returned to the College to her music course. Without Ade and his clarinet.

* * *

Mr Allen and Miss Goltz continued with their study of the Mozart Trio. But he was aware that she seemed preoccupied with something other than the music they were practising.. Suddenly she said:

'You see Mr Allen it's just a question of connecting things.' She reached out and took the carving. 'Just look at this musician. It was carved by a Yoruba craftsman who actually came to England and studied here for several years before returning. Look at the quality of the wood, unvarnished. The rectangular body with the geometrical patterning, the face with full lips, and the lips and clarinet ….it's some sort of clarinet I believe. Difficult to say whether the styling is European or African. I don't think it matters really. Just its beautiful symmetry and clarity ..nothing bulbous or crude. Nor Grecian, like some of the Ife bronzes. Those heavy sad eyelids. And the feet, so … grounded. But the music which is coming from it, from the wood, the lips, through the clarinet with its those regular grooves and flutings, has a kind of organic unity, even though of course it is quite mute. The feeling behind it is….enhanced by the precision of the carving.'

Mr Allen was silenced by this long dissertation. Eventually he said: 'Yes I can see what you mean. Beautiful. Were you given it by a friend? Or were you in Africa?'

'It was a friend. A musician. He played the clarinet too. Just like this one.'

* * *

For several weeks Margaret heard nothing from Ade. Then there were two or three letters. It was suggested that things might be improving. He missed her terribly. Then silence. Several of her letters were unanswered. She scanned the papers, sought out foreign news, even phoned the Nigerian Embassy. Gradually over several weary months a story came out of fierce fighting close to the area where he had lived. Then of a massacre. Only another year later was she able to establish the extent of the killing and the near-certainty that Ade and the rest of his family had been included.

By now her calendar was covered with a fair number of dates for concerts accompanying lieder singers, violinists. And occasional chamber music sessions, but never with a clarinet. But musically and within herself she was still in a kind of limbo.

One morning, a year or so later, there was a message from the Royal College.

'A parcel for you, Miss Goltz. We didn't have an address, but someone gave us your number.'

'Where is it from?'

'Can't quite say Miss. A Nigerian dropped it off here.'

'A Nigerian? Did he give his name?'

'No. He was just passing. Delivering it for a friend.'

As soon as she picked up the parcel she thought she recognised the writing on it. At home in her new flat in Kensington she opened it and held the clarinettist in her two hands. There was short note from Ade, written a year earlier, telling her that he had bought it from the wood carver on his way through Ibadan. He wasn't quite sure how he would get the carving to her, if he didn't bring it to her himself. 'Once things have settled down, I will be back. I promise.' The note said nothing specifically about the war. There was no explanation for the year's delay in delivery.

When she had first slept with Ade she had been anxious not to conceive. She told herself that she had not been prepared for a baby yet. But now she wished she had had a baby. Having the beautiful wooden figure standing on the piano was as close as she could get to mothering Ade's child.

* * *

'Yes it was a friend. A dear friend. We played that Kegelstatt trio you know. He gave me this carving. He came from Africa.' Looking at Miss Goltz, Mr Allen was able to see that she was wrapped in thought. But she didn't seem, as far as he could tell, to be upset or moved by the admission except in a very distant way.. An oddly severe, detached kind of person really. Not giving anything away. Perhaps she was not one to dwell unnecessarily on memories.

Strange, how every time she looked at the carving she saw its connectedness. The music pouring directly from the wooden centre of the figure, through the chest, the throat, the mouth, and the lips into the stubby clarinet. And she could hear its music. Precise, fluent, responsive. And certainly heavenly. After all it was Mozart. And there was too the sound of her own piano playing: teasing, questioning and answering. Yes certainly, a marriage made in heaven.

THE BARRIER

'With any other vehicle,' he said to himself, 'there would be the danger of getting bogged down.' He wiped away a trickle of sweat and dust which was creeping down from his forehead to his eyebrows. 'But not with this one. As long as I keep up the speed.'

Here and there patches of an almost white sand encroached on the road. On either side a meagre covering of spindly plants ran right up to a bare rocky escarpment in the middle distance, partly obscured by heat haze and dust. At this rate he would make Timbou in three hours. Time for a quick meal and a drink before the mining equipment people's plane dropped in at the makeshift runway. A quick show round and some discussion of the sort of machinery they were looking for. An hour or so should be enough; they wouldn't want to hang about. Everyone away by mid afternoon. He himself would be back at Zander by the evening. It couldn't be easier. Unless something turned up to put things out. Of course there was no guarantee, in a country as empty and undeveloped as this, that things might not go wrong. Unexplained delays, missing documents, the wrong person in the wrong place, an unseasonal rainstorm. Or a simple breakdown in the communications systems. And there was also the political aspect. The militias had been active on this route last year. However, intelligence said they had moved eastwards again.

The driver pushed the vehicle along a little faster. He was getting like the others, worrying too much, looking for trouble. People could be very jumpy. Exaggerate the dangers. Take this journey: he had intended to take a driver with him, in case of breakdowns. But at the last minute nobody was available and he was secretly rather pleased. A trip like this was always more enjoyable when he was on his own, he thought. Though some would have said he was taking an unnecessary risk. Good job he had the 4.2 litre Toyota though. Safer, quicker. And a much more enjoyable drive. No one else on the road. A steady forty or fifty. He felt the wheels beginning to wander a little as he cut through an invading tongue of sand. A deliberately provocative twist on the wheel made the vehicle slew even further, so that he could accelerate out of it. No problem.

Ahead the road climbed over a low shoulder in the escarpment, then dipped down to a flat plain between several piles of massive boulders. There was a well here, and a couple of huts. Today he could see a herd of twenty or thirty cattle and several herdsmen. Apparently waiting.

Then he saw the barrier. A pole across the road, weighted on one end, and a shabbily dressed man with what looked like a gun. He slowed the vehicle down expecting the barrier would be raised. The man did not move a muscle. Bringing the vehicle to a halt only inches from the bar, the driver clambered out and said to the man: 'Tabou. Okay?' And lifted his hands, miming the opening of the barrier.

The man shook his head. 'No Tabou today,' he said.

'Why not?'

The man shook his head again, obviously not understanding, but repeating the words. 'No Tabou.'

It was really quite silly. The barrier only crossed the place where there was the road. It would have been perfectly possible to have swung either to the right or left of the barrier, and bump through on the rough land on either side. Even the gun was a joke…he could see it was a huntsman's gun, a shakabulla, which would hardly have dented the cars wings, much less bring the vehicle to a halt. He started to get back in when suddenly someone a voice came to him, as if from above his head.

'I'm afraid the road is closed. You cannot travel to Tabou today, not on this road.' He turned round, curious because of the apparent elevation of the voice.

Standing just behind the car was a white horse and on its back a man dressed in long blue gown, a white and purple headdress and a deeper blue scarf over the bottom part of his face. There were tassels and bits of finery hanging from the horse's flanks and neck.

'If you have to go to Tabou, better take the other route.'

'Look here, I'm from the mining company. I have an appointment there in three hours. I can't afford to go back and take the other road.'

The man looked at him, as if trying to weigh up something. Then he said:

'Whatever you decide to do, this particular road is not open.'

'Why not?'

'That I am not at liberty to divulge.'

'Is it mined?

'That is not the point …but no, no mines as yet.'

'Militia?'

'I'm afraid I can't say.'

'But they can't just close a road.'

The horseman shrugged. Even with the weight of his chunky Toyota next to him, the driver still felt the disadvantage of having to look up at the rider.

To hide his frustration he took a pair of binoculars from the car, walked over to one of the piles of rocks and clambered up to the top. With his mobile phone he tried to make contact with the firm back in Zander. He knew it would be useless. He tried to get through the mine people at Tabou … they might know who was behind all this. But no joy there either. He even scanned the skyline with his binoculars, but saw nothing suspicious. He climbed down the hill & then stood there, studying the lie of the land, the sand and vegetation on either side of the barrier. Deliberate, unhurried, as if to say, well I can be just as cool and remote as you, Mister Horseman.

When he got back to his car again, he saw that the horseman, still mounted, was also on his mobile phone. He had taken the scarf away from his face. Quite young, fresh-faced, but still very calm and unflustered. And already the driver had noted how well spoken he was.

The call made, he said: 'I have spoken with the people involved. There is no question of the road being opened at the moment. Of course if you wait say three or four hours they say it may be possible. They stress: *may* be possible. I cannot…'

'Oh come on!' the driver interrupted. 'By then I will have missed my appointment.'

'So I suggest you proceed back to the junction, and then take the old road. You will be delayed but by not much more than a couple of hours or so.'

'And that road's clear then?'

'As far as I am aware. But I can offer no guarantees.'

'Great!' It was impossible to disguise his annoyance, although he could see that it made no impression on the horseman.

'Well, and who are you, then?' the driver said abruptly, changing his tack.

'Myself you mean?'

'Yourself and the people who put you up to this.'

'I can't speak for those people, since I am not one of them. I have just told you that the road is closed, in order to protect you from any inconvenience. However I am Faisal.' He reached into his gown and drew out a wallet, and handed the driver a card. There was a name, a mobile phone number, and then a box number in Zander. He looked at the card and said: 'Well at least it means I know who I can blame for this …obstruction. When I speak to the authorities.' He placed the card behind the windscreen.

The man smiled and inclined his head slightly before beginning to turn his horse away. Then he stopped and looked back at the driver.

'I don't wish to be …officious or inhospitable…but I was noticing that you were inspecting the ground on either side of the barrier. I am sure that splendid vehicle of yours would be able to cope with its undulations quite adequately. However, I advise you to take my word for it. The road is indeed closed. Good day sir.'

'And good day to you too. Thank you very much for everything.'

The driver got back into the Toyota and revved it fiercely, as if he were contemplating crashing through the barrier and proceeding on his journey. Then he wrenched the wheel and made a huge turn, riffling up the dust in a great cloud, the wheels skidding but still holding, until he was facing the way back to Zander. The horseman was nowhere to be seen.

As the driver climbed the low escarpment he saw ahead a cloud of dust. More then one vehicle was coming towards him and making heavy weather of the road. As they approached they swung onto the rough ground, and continued their bucking and bouncing path towards the well and the barrier. Two battered Peugeot saloon cars, one without a front bumper, but both heavily laden with passengers, the second with women and children inside, so that the underside and exhaust were scraping the sand. Smoke poured ominously from the back. Neither vehicle was going to be able to continue on the path they were following for much longer. He stopped his vehicle and looked back at the drama.

They had reached the well, about a hundred metres from the barrier, and were forging on. It was clear that they had no intention of stopping. He laughed out loud.

'Typical,' he said to himself. 'Here I am, perfectly law-abiding, even on semi-official business, properly set up with a roadworthy vehicle, and I let myself be put off by some guy on horseback.' He crashed his fist onto the dashboard. 'Whereas these guys, don't stop to ask. They just get on and do it.'

By now the two Peugeots had bounced and skidded their way back to the main track beyond the feeble barrier and were accelerating away again towards Tabou.

'Perhaps I should have followed in their wake, so to speak,' he said to himself with a shrug. But he continued on his journey back to the junction and the old road, ashamed to be seen to change his mind again on account of these careless travellers.

* * *

His arrival at Tabou was two hours later than planned. The skies were hazy and there was a drop in temperature and a chilling breeze and harmattan mist drifted down from the desert escarpment. The machinery people who had flown in earlier were clearly annoyed by the delay, but the business was conducted quickly and seamlessly. At four o'clock it was all done and their plane took off again, they having turned down his offer of a meal.

But no reason why he shouldn't have a quick meal. He left the mine and drove into the town, a scatter of breeze block and grass buildings on either side of a wide sandy avenue. The place was deserted except for a few slinking dogs and one woman carrying water. But the one café-restaurant there, owned by an Algerian, had a good reputation. There were several tables under umbrellas in front, in bright yellow green and red stripes. A huge television aerial stood on a post. Although it was an odd time of day to be eating a meal, the boy took his order, and brought some bottled water. Five minutes after he had started his food, the Algerian came out to ask him if everything was okay.

'You come up from Zander?

'That's right.'

'On the old road of course.'

'Well actually yes, why?'

'You haven't seen the news? Trouble on the other road.'

'What kind of trouble?'

'Just come inside. You can see it on the TV. I'll bring your table in.' There was a news programme, a local reporter. The driver recognised immediately the stretch of country where he had been stopped by the barrier. The cameras were following an army vehicle. Then there were two vehicles, probably Peugeots, blackened smoking heaps. One without a front bumper. By the side of one vehicle there were three bodies stretched out on the sand. Then the camera moved alongside the second vehicle, three or four bodies, one a woman, two at least children. 'Sensible of you to come on the other road, the old one. Did someone warn you?'

'Yes they did,' he said trying to disguise the shake in his voice.' Yes, they warned me.'

He hurried the rest of his meal and started on the homeward journey. The Algerian reported that it was safe, especially now the army were around. He would in fact be met by an army escort for the last part of the journey. He drove slowly, frequently scanning the road ahead and on both sides. The dust behind the vehicle left him with no view behind. Plenty of time to think, though. What if he had proceeded, driven round that makeshift barrier, would they have cut him down, just like that? Although his Toyota was probably a match in terms of speed for the militias pickups, he had no idea what weaponry these people had. Would they have been more wary of picking off an official looking vehicle like his? With a European on board? Who knows? The horseman had after all warned him.

The visiting card was still tucked behind the windscreen. He reached for it, and without looking at it, threw it out of the window. In his wing mirror he saw it tumble and flicker before it was swallowed up by the dust in the wake of the vehicle. And when eventually he saw the army escort unit ahead of him, and a soldier waved him down, he felt a surge of relief.

SEA NEVER DRY

Leaning on the hotel's veranda rail, he looks down at the opaque Lagoon waters. Two crabs scuttle along the shallows and hide in the reeds. Across the water the city skyline hovers above rafts of floating timber, coils of weed, and the sweet smells of sewage, diesel and decay. A dual carriageway, aloof on stilts above a scrap-iron yard, slices down to the water and then hurls itself into the clutter of downtown housing. Cars and vans pursue the green city buses. Out-of-town trucks with multi-coloured wooden superstructures, …they are called 'bolakajas,' it means 'get-down-and-fight' so Elizabeth told him …..trundle towards the bus parks and markets. Inscriptions are scrawled above their cabs, or along the rainbow-coloured wooden side-panels. Some are in local languages, but there are the homely English ones too: 'The Lord is My Sheppard, Honestly the Best Policy, God Save!' There was one last week: 'Sea Never Dry'.

Yellow and green taxis vie with cars and vans and cyclists as they all scurry and plunge into the crush of shanty housing. Over the washing lines and corrugated iron roofs, the ornate profiles of a few Brazilian-style villas. And then further back, the uncertain majesty of the Anglican Cathedral, two mosques and the skeletal glass and concrete of new office blocks, Government Departments and International Banks, delineated as sharp as marquetry under the first bubbles of wet-season cumulus.

He walks round to the south facing wing of the hotel, overlooking dunes and then the Atlantic. From here he can see a faint stripe of yellow sand, deep blue ocean and a skim of surf. Where, six months ago, Elizabeth and he walked, and traded what they had to offer. Advice and endorsement from him…other consolations from her. And now six months later, she just doesn't answer the phone. Okay she's a busy woman, but she could at least ring him back.

* * *

It was one of those consultation exercises when you feel in your bones that no one will really be taking you seriously. Not that that was a problem. Whatever was decided the firm at least would be paid. The main shipping channel through the sand barrier from the open Atlantic to the lagoon had to be kept clear of silt. Three or four vessels worked tirelessly ….well as long as there were funds ….to keep it open especially at the seaward end, but it was clearly a losing battle. The oblique Atlantic surf and the deep water just off shore ensured that millions of tons of silt were swept along the coast as long shore drift. The accumulation of silt was far in excess of anything that even a dozen dredgers could make any impression on. Mclintocks, for whom he was one of the consultants, had some expertise in dealing with this kind of problem. They would make recommendations. He was to spend a week in the country investigating and then report back to head office.

On his arrival he made contact with their firm's resident representative Mike Prosser. 'Nice to have you with us, John. Now, you're going to need to talk to the Junior Minister for Reconstruction. I've fixed it up for you to meet her tomorrow, okay?' The surprise he felt on hearing that there was a woman in charge of such a department must have shown in his face. 'Yes! Lizzie, the Minister, just come back from America. A PhD in Development Economics, several years with a Wall Street bank. And if you ask me, too clever by half. Don't underestimate our Lizzie old boy. And whatever you do don't call her Lizzie! It's Minister, okay?'

'She sounds …..young then.'

Mike laughed. 'You wait and see.'

The next day he was ushered into the Minister's office. She was standing looking out of the windows overlooking the city. Wow! he said to myself. Slender. Graceful. She turned to him. And came forward to offer a hand to shake. The blackest of black skins, no hint of dark brown, hair pulled back tightly from her forehead, dark sparkling audacious eyes, an expressive mouth. A business suit that managed to look decorative as well as businesslike. And for a few seconds he thought to himself: whatever battle you might have to fight here, you will lose it. But, golly, who wouldn't relish such a defeat!

Not that she gave him time to admire her. She'd allowed him about twenty seconds for that, then it was as if she clicked her fingers in his face, and they were sitting down and right onto the matter of the sea-lane. He went through the information he had so far, quantities of silt, local currents, and long-shore drift, projected rates of accumulation, the efficiency of current dredging methods. She took it all in. At one point, someone came in with some papers but she sent him scuttling away.

'I told you. No interruptions.'

Then the telephone rang and she apologised to him, turned to face the window again, and spoke to someone, this time deferentially. Meanwhile he could look at her once again, this time in profile. The line from her hair, through cheek, chin, neck, then shoulder, slim back and hip was breath-taking.

The phone call over, she turned back to him.

'What do you think?' she said.

Flustered he said foolishly: 'Think of what?' A ghost of a smile on her lips?

'What do you think will be the best solution to our silt problem here. Whatever happens, this port of ours needs to be able to take bigger and bigger vessels.'

And then he launched into his best presentation mode. He listed a whole series of people he needed to consult. The Minister put reading glasses on and ticked things off on a sheet on her desk…it looked identical with his own suggested list. 'Okay. I'll arrange all these. Well most of them. Don't expect a full house. People can sometimes be very evasive. But I can get you started tomorrow with the Port Authority. That's been arranged already.'

He shrugged. 'Thanks.' Who was being evasive? At least there was one here who wasn't. Then she caught him out again.

'Okay. Any preliminary thoughts. Solutions?'

'Well it would be foolish…..'

'Come on Mr Foster. Have some courage. I'm not recording this.' She looked at her desk vaguely. 'Well not as far as I can tell?' She smiled radiantly: 'Can I call you John? You don't mind.'

'Yes that's fine,' ….and after a minute's hesitation … 'Minister.' Apparently no kind of reciprocation on names.

'You were going to tell me about the possible solutions.'

'Well it is of course early…..' and she peered at him over her glasses, like a schoolmisteress, and he forged on. 'It's all a question of length of term,' He said. 'Whether you go for five years or twenty-five. Simple short term answer, stick a great pipe here, on the mud flats, and pump the stuff across the sea channel to the eastern flats. Cost. God knows, but we'll make some kind of guess eventually. Certainly a few millions. Alternatively: we go to the sea itself. The whole stretch of coast, off this map altogether. Groins and barriers, so that the whole l.s.d. problem is diverted completely and onto someone else's doorstep.

'By l.s.d. of course you don't mean the money?'

'No. Sorry. Long shore drift. But a proper reclamation scheme would make the access to the lagoon permanent. And incidentally create a lot of land for development several miles along the coast. Tourism, Industrial, you name it. South of France, Rhone delta, salt lagoons, flamingos, futuristic hotel resorts. Quite apart from the infrastructure you'd need to run it.'

'Sounds quite ….progressive, forward-looking?'

'Well, I'm probably letting my imagination run away with me…'

'How much?'

'You mean imagination? No, I see. Money? Oh, impossible to give an estimate…..'

'Come on John. Courage.'

'Hundreds of millions. At least ten times the other more modest one.'

She took off her glasses and looked at him, as if weighing something up. Then her final question, which took him just as much by surprise.

'So, what are you doing this afternoon?'

'Nothing in particular?'

'Well let's go and have a look at it.'

'You mean …the sea-channel and the coast?' He pictured them sweeping over in a ministerial helicopter, the Minister's head leaning close to his, the wind ruffling their clothes, and her scent making him dizzy.

'You're at the Plaza? You can manage without a siesta can't you. I'll pick you up at the sea front entrance at two. It'll be a blue Mercedes.' And then with the slightest of nods, he was whisked away.

By two thirty they were spinning along the coast road in the open top Mercedes. He sat in the back with the Minister while she chatted with the ministerial chauffeur in a mixture of English and a local language. He could see he was tickled pink by what she had to say. Suddenly she pointed across the carriageway to an opening in the sea wall, and they turned sharply onto soft sand. No further, the chauffeur said, or we stuck.

The Minister plucked her high heel shoes off, and leapt out onto the sand. 'Come on,' she said. 'We need to walk from here. You stay, brother driver. Don't let the thieves steal my lovely blue car!' Then she loosened her hair from its clips and band so that it swung free, just slightly African, but with modest waves, across neck and shoulders.

The driver looked at him and shook his head as if to say: 'She's mad As a hatter. Or whatever creature symbolises madness in this country.'

They walked across the level sands between a scatter of Corsican pine, and some decaying prickly pear. The Minister was in high spirits and moved faster than he did with his heavy shoes, unwilling to commit myself to barefoot walking. Eventually they came up to a ridge overlooking the sea. The sands swept down in a dangerous curve, onto which the arrow straight surf came cruising in and crashed in great loops of green water curdled with surf. At the foot of this slope stood several women, some standing in the shallows, others kneeling on the sand itself, all dressed in white, holding their hands up to the skies, and forwards as if pleading with the sea, asking the sea whether they might embrace it. They sang, tunelessly but insistent, almost as if they were weeping for some lost child or a remote paradise.

'The stupid women,' the Minister said beside him. 'What are they trying to do? Stop the waves?'

'I suppose it's something religious,' he said.

'Superstition. Some sect who worship the sea. Madness if you ask me. What can they do?' And it was clear that the Minister was upset. 'Come this way,' she shouted above the sound of the surf and the women wailing. We walked towards the sea-channel. A small vessel could be seen negotiating the channel.

'So John. Tell me again what you have in mind. And don't worry. No one will misquote you. I'm not wired up!'

And he did his bit again. Quite exhilarating. To lecture in front of the sand and sea and sky about how he planned to tame them, Especially with Lizzie watching. Unfortunately, that was when the more intimate word came out.... 'Just look across there, Lizzie, where the shipping channel begins to curve round.' And she looked at him and smiled. He was okay with the impertinence.

Once he'd finished, she said. 'This pipe, You know, the cheap option. Who would install it?'

'You could employ one of the big companies, Taylor, or

Puskoff. But there are local firms I'm sure who could have a go at it. As long as you had a good plan.'

'And the other one. Who does that?'

'You mean the one with the tourism and development potential? Oh. You'd have to go world wide for that.'

'No chance for the locals.'

'No chance. In fact,' he said glumly, 'You'd need one of the big boys, like de Koening. Do you know of him?'

'Sure.'

'Well, this is right up his street. Mind you, he would bring in a lot of his own labour and infrastructure. Locals would hardly get a look in. But it would all be good for development potential in the long term.'

'Absolutely John. And for those big greedy International companies involved. But what we need here is a practical solution for *us* today that will be good for our economy *now*.'

'That's one way of looking at it.'

'Anyhow. You'll make your recommendations.'

'I shall. Quite objectively. Short term, long term.'

As you must John. Right. Seen enough? We'd better get back home before that driver starts to think we've run off without him.'

And she ran and skipped back to the car at her usual lick, with him struggling along behind her.

On the drive back into the city, she sat just that little bit closer to me, and flicked her bare toes here and there to emphasize points in her explanations about the importance of local employment and contract opportunities. Then they were approaching the hotel, and she hastily did up her hair, pushed her feet into the shoes, and drew back her shoulders, pinched her nostrils, as if to resume her Ministerial persona.

She gave him no time to thank her for the trip.

'Where do you eat tonight?' she said.

'In the hotel, I suppose.'

'How absolutely awful. Look, be ready at seven. Wait in your room. The driver will pick you up at seven.'

'But where.....I mean what kind of dress?'

'Just casual. But decent. You're eating at my place. Do you like steak?' But she hardly waited for any answer. As if his response was predictable.

The Mercedes called for him at seven. It was the same driver. 'I hope you enjoyed the afternoon fresh air sir.' He looked at him but there was no hint of familiarity. The Minister's house was in a Government suburb and access was through a gated entrance with security guards. They stopped at a flamboyant Californian style villa and he was ushered in. There seemed to be a lot of people bustling about, but a uniformed servant took him into a room at the side and told him that the Minister would be with him shortly. He offered him a drink from a corner bar, and he took a beer. Then as he sank back in a floundering heap of cushions, he tried to admire the generous supply of African carvings and tapestries, and the bookcases heaving with classics and biographies, but with American literature well represented.

When the Minister came in she was wearing an off-the shoulder red dress. Flame red. Her hair was arranged much more artily. He staggered up from the cushions and she held his hand to enable him to stay upright.

'Sorry to be so long, John. These wretched people. They give me no peace.'

'It's alright,' he said. 'Work can be very ……demanding.'

'It can, but only so far. Ten minutes more and then these people get their marching orders. Then we can enjoy our evening together. Excuse me again…' and she was out of the door. He picked up a huge book on African Art and was just beginning to wade through it when she was back.

'That's it. They've all gone. Come into the sitting room. Food will be ready in half an hour.'

They chatted about life in London. She wanted to know about the theatre, a subject on which he was badly informed. She forbade any talk of work or politics. But his home and other places in the world where he had worked in came up for discussion. She asked after his two children, his divorced wife. She in turn told him about her home town in the Nigerian Mid-west, her English education, her recent American experience. Of the Americans in general she was very disparaging, even though ….not that he mentioned this …she had a pleasantly disarming American accent herself.

The other thing that was worrying him was the lack of other guests. He had always supposed that Ministers, even when they were out of the public eye, dined in style with several guests. But there was no one else here. And through the arch which led to a garden terrace he could see a candle-lit table laid for two.

And then dinner was served. Everything was well done. Including the wine. She apologised for it being 'only Californian' but it was certainly excellent. But the servant who dispensed it filled up his glass too frequently so that he lost all idea of how much he had drunk. Later they sat on another huge bamboo settle with cushions, not very intimate since they were probably a couple of yards apart. There were liquors or whisky. Background music: Vivaldi. Making a strange counterpoint with the buzz of the crickets and the hum of the air-conditioning.

The Minister…… no, he was back with the name Lizzie again…… suddenly sprang up, rang a bell and called in the two servants, and also the cook. 'That was fine, wasn't it John. So, now, the three of you, scoot. I don't want to see you until tomorrow morning.'

They all bowed and made their departure, shutting the dining room doors.

'Now,' said Lizzie. 'More to drink?'

He risked another whisky resolving it would be his last. She brought it to him and sat now next to me on the bamboo armchair. She laid her head back on the cushion next to his shoulder, took his hand, and held it to her cheek. It only required him to incline his head a few inches to slide a hand behind her head, for his lips to come into direct contact with her shoulder, and then up to her lips. It was a long long kiss. 'That's better' she said. She took his hand, led him off the veranda, and into another annexe or sitting room of some kind, and pulled on a cord which closed the blinds. There was light reflected through the purple blinds, and a high window, but it was difficult to see clearly. Then she was holding him again and undoing the buttons of his shirt. They seemed to be lost on a vast prairie of cushions, but it ceased to be important to understand its geography.

Lizzie woke him at about half-six. She was wearing a white housecoat. 'Sorry chum,' she said. 'Breakfast in bed and then you'll have to go. Well, by eight.'

She disappeared into the dining room, and as he lay back he

heard the clatter of a coffee maker, and plates, the opening of the fridge. Then she came back with a tray coffee, fresh milk, and rolls and butter. A smaller toaster. Some boxes of cereals. They lounged in bed close to each other, feeding each other bits of rolls, and toast, and rice crispies. Then as they pushed away the tray, she nuzzled into his shoulder again, and her hand was on his chest.

'John, darling. You know your report.'

'Yes,' he said, struggling to remember quite which report she was talking about.

'Well, do you think you could sort of emphasize the advantages to our economy, employment, etc of that first alternative. The limited objective.'

'The pipe, you mean.'

'Absolutely. You see, I am a politician, and I do have to think what is best for my country, don't I?'

'I suppose so. But you've got to consider that the alternative, the big scheme, would in the long run be better for the country. It would be a real developmental step forward.'

She still was tracing her finger over his chest, as if speculatively. 'John now, please think what I'm saying. Okay. The pipe is IN. de Koening or whoever he is, that style Development plan is OUT.'

'But I can't ....lie.'

'Nor should you darling. Integrity is your watchword, I know. I love you for it. But there are ways of presenting things aren't there? Enthusiasm slightly veiled, a dismissal made sweet with apologies. You know how to do it.'

'Well I suppose I do.'

'Well do it then okay. For my sake.'

'And for the country's sake too?'

'That goes without saying.'

It was suggested that he leave before eight. And the chauffeur's car met him at the tradesman's entrance. The driver was respectful as always. No hint of a sly look, or a twitch at the corner of the mouth.

Of course he knew what had happened to him. And when that next day all his visits and consultations went like clockwork, it merely reinforced his willingness to bend the words he would use in his report. A few day's later, there was a reception in Lizzie's house. Well, the Minister's house. It was strange to be treated like a formal guest where previously he had been a clandestine lover.

The Minister presented him to a dozen or so African chiefs, senior civil servants, a few academics (politically involved) and someone who was described as an up-and-coming novelist And then there was de Koehning himself, apparently on a visit from Europe and America. A huge untidy man, loud and arrogant, puffing on a damp cigar even though it had been suggested that smoking should be done on the veranda. He spoke to Lizzie as if she were a slightly precocious schoolgirl, and smiled maliciously whenever the local economy came into the conversation, as if no one there was likely to do any good, it being beyond repair. John caught Lizzie's eye once or twice and there was a brief closing of the eyes & shaking of the head, as if to say 'How unutterably awful. What cretins! If only we could ……' But the reception ground on, and he made his way round another bevy of business men, a bishop, and several wives who were difficult to place. One thing was clear; people like de Koehning might look down on Lizzie, but the wives were mostly in awe of her. When the reception was over Lizzie managed to steer him into the garden as the rest of the guests left. Lizzie seemed slightly ill at ease.

'What's up?' he said, as they curled up together on the bamboo thing.'

'I can't get that horrible man out of my mind,' Lizzie said.

'Oh forget about him, Lizzie.'

'Make me!' she said.

He had to leave at twelve that night for some reason of protocol. The chauffeur was there at the tradesman's entrance with his car and polite smile.

During the rest of the week he only met Lizzie fleetingly, and always in public. She had whispered to him about an arrangement for the two of them on his last night in the country, but then at six she rang him, full of apologies. 'I have to meet with these ministers in the North, tomorrow morning. Travel this evening. Isn't it dreadful? I'm not going to see you at all.'

'That's awful,' he said.

'When will you be coming back here, John?'

'In a few months time, especially if, 'you know what' comes off in the way we were talking.'

'Well it will come off, won't it, darling? You put in your report didn't you.'

'I have to put it in tonight.'

He heard an intake of breath. 'I thought that it had already …you know…gone in.'

'As good as …' I said.

'And you did recommend things the way we suggested. You know, for the good of the country and all that?'

'Absolutely, although ….'

'Although? Look, darling, it's very important for me, politically, that I know how things stand.'

'Don't worry. I did what you asked.'

'Darling, I love you. I'm devastated that you're going. Come back soon. Write to me as soon as you get home.'

'Okay.'

'And ….give my best regards to your children.'

'I will….'

'And your ex-wife too if …….'

'If I see her.'

'But from the Minister, eh!' There were the explosions of two blown kisses in the earpiece.

* * *

Six months has elapsed and he is back. Before he left London they said that there was still considerable interest in their pipeline scheme, but not much action. More detailed investigations to be undertaken, preliminary interviews with prospective contractors. While he was away, phone calls between himself Lizzie were a pretty desultory business, together with confusing e-mails from Lizzie in a strangely distant tone. Were they perhaps dictated to a secretary.? The Minister was busy travelling to America, to other African states, or involved in important government business. He was never quite clear where she was and what she was doing.

Looking across the lagoon at the city skyline, he wonders where he and Lizzie stand. The message he sent to her office, announcing his return, doesn't seem to have had much effect. Of course Lizzie was using him, he knew that. But surely it was all in a good cause. The two schemes, each has its good and bad points. For the country. So making it clear in his report which scheme he favoured, was not really hurting anyone and made Lizzie happy. She knows he's back in the country, why doesn't she ring him

When the phone actually rings, his heartbeat accelerates. But it is only Mike.

'Welcome back. Can I come round and see you?' He sounds very tired. Half an hour later, when he comes in, he looks a bit grey too. Along with the usual expatriate yellowing. He sits down with a beer. 'Bad news,' he says.

'Oh yes,' he says, hardly listening, still anxious about getting in touch with Lizzie.

'The pipeline,' says Mike. 'It's off!'

'How do you mean? Off?'

'They've changed their minds. You know what they're like.'

'So why I am here?'

'Sorry old man. Only let me know yesterday. Too late to warn you, or put you off coming.'

'So what happens now.'

'They're going all out for that big Marine Development Project, you know. Billions it'll cost them. And it's going to be de Koehning's baby. Who knows whether it'll work.'

He sits, wondering what all this will mean for Lizzie. And how to ask. Eventually he says, as if revealing a confidence on which he has special insight.

'Well, to be honest, I think there was, and is, a lot to be said for that big Development Project. In the long term. I told that minister….'

'You mean Lizzie? Come on, John. Don't be shy. We knew

there was something going on there between you two.'

'Nonsense. Just a couple of meals.'

'I told you to be careful about her didn't I.'

'No reason…..'

'Anyhow. Problem solved as far as you're concerned.'

'You mean. This pipeline contract?'

'That as well. But I meant Lizzie. Didn't you see it in the papers. Huge event. Plastered across half the pages. She and de Koehning.'

'Doing what ……?'

'Getting married. Don't ask me what it means when people like Lizzie and that big ape get married. Business as usual?' Fortunately, Mike is too fed up by the failure of the pipeline project to notice the shock of his news to his colleague's system.

But is it a shock? Emotionally yes. But perhaps he is prepared for it. What Lizzie and he 'traded' back then was merely what they had to hand. It was obviously never anything very profound for her. He has still to decide what it all meant to him.

Those women wading in the surf, throwing their hands in the air, wailing. Perhaps if he'd bothered to ask them, they would have warned him. Unless they were in league with Lizzie all the time.

He looks down at the lagoon waters. One rather smaller crab lurches by one of the veranda supports when a big purple one suddenly pounces on it, tries to throttle it until they both scuttle back to the deeper water and the reeds. The smaller crab would have done the same to the bigger one, if he had been a bit bigger and had the ambush advantage of the hiding place, he thinks.

BETWEEN COURSES

The Japanese girl was studying the menu outside as Mariella and I went in. We had just bundled Week One onto the train. The next batch of 'punters' as Mariella called them were not expected for a couple of hours. I had suggested this place to eat on the chance that it would be livelier. Mariella as our driver and painting course organiser had not ceased to babble on throughout the hour's lurching journey in the minibus from La Caccia into the city.

But I was out of luck. The restaurant was unusually quiet, lots of empty tables, and an intimate atmosphere. 'Quiet here,' she said. As if it were a disqualification. 'Hope the food's okay. After a week of that stuff at Catch, I could do with something better.'

I said nothing. It took me a moment to recognise her abbreviation of the name of the country house we were staying in. As the person responsible for things at La Caccia from accommodation to transport, from easels to tubes of paint, wasn't the quality of the food also part of her brief? And it had been awful. The brochure had raved about Italian farmhouse cuisine. Everyone there, including the cook, was pleasantness itself, but all the staff came from Eastern Europe and the service was slow, the food insipid.

'Difficult to get proper staff, you know,' she said as we settled down to our bruschetta. 'I didn't like to say anything to that lot on the bus. Seemed happy enough. Probably haven't a clue what to expect.'

I almost said that she was lucky because they were too polite to complain. They had been a good party, friendly, eager, responsive, though one or two inevitably were fairly clueless. They had all enjoyed the trips out, and the sketching and the painting, when they had the chance to do any.

'Perhaps the staff'll have settled down this week. Getting their bearings,' I offered.

'Well getting their bearings is what they bloody better do. Or they'll be out on their necks, you see if they're not.'

Just the right atmosphere for a Painting course in Tuscany, I thought.

Just then over Mariella's shoulder, I saw the Japanese girl sit down at a corner table, close to the window. She was perhaps in her twenties, though I couldn't be sure. Smart jeans, a small short purple jacket with lacey edging, and a pink blouse. Hair tied back in a kind of bun. She placed a camera and a small notebook on the table beside her and began to study the menu.

Meanwhile Mariella was tucking into her pasta and talking about the Week Two party that we were due to collect from the station.

'Pretty disheartening for you, Paul...a real artist like yourself, stuck with the same weary band of wrinklies hoping to become landscape artists in one week flat. Beats me where they get the idea from.'

But wasn't that what the brochure had, against my advice, implied?

'I think a few of them were pretty proficient already you know. It's not as if they come here empty-handed.'

'But so limited. I mean, all they seem to want is to paint castellos on hill tops sunflowers and a line of those pointy trees.'

'Well I suppose we all have our own romantic picture of

Tuscany. After all it seemed to work for the masters.'

'Come off it, Paul. Most of our lot would be better off painting flowers and garden gnomes in their prim little back gardens.' She pushed her plate away, picked up the carafe and squinted at the wine level in it before ordering another. Behind her I saw the Japanese girl pick up her camera and inspect the window where a clambering plant was trying to curl its way into the room. She studied it, then took a photograph. Now she looked down at the table top, adjusted the cutlery, the small vase of flowers and pointed the camera at the table setting, changed her mind, readjusted, then took another picture. Although it was shaded in the room there appeared to be no flash. She made a careful note in her notebook.

'Anyhow, let's hope that those builders have finished with the extension by the end of next week. I've got six more booked up as well as the usual twelve Keep us all busy and the money rolling in.'

'Actually Mariella that was something I wanted to ask you about.'

'You mean the money? End of the week okay with you?' I was about to protest that the money was not in my mind but then our main courses arrived. 'What vegetables are these?' she asked the waiter, her mouth drooping wearily as she half listened to his polite explanations about availability.

'Typical!' she said as he left.

I tried to forget her rudeness. 'You were saying that next week we would have eighteen students. Isn't that going to be difficult for me to get round to see them all at work properly.'

'No problemo. I'll take half off to the beach or some hill-top town while you do your stuff with the others.'

'But I think it's important that they work as a single group. Connecting the visits and the sketching with the work we do in the garden and the studio.'

'You're the boss, Paul. Keep them all together then.'

'But how on earth do I keep tabs on….?'

'Don't worry, Paul. These people are just happy to be here in Tuscany, and to have a real artist in front of them. Italian food, decent wine, and bob's your uncle. Assuming those people back at Catch get their finger out. Look if you're worried about it I'll put in for an extra 20% on your fee…'

'That's not what I meant.'

'Right, I tell you what, why don't I come in and help you out. I did quite a bit of Art in my Media Studies. Not of course up to your standard…'

The Japanese girl's first course came to her table. She thanked the waiter, then studied it, a half-smile on her face. She rotated the plate two or three times, put her head slightly to one side, then selected a view, and took one picture, then zoomed in for a closer Notebook again. Then she sat back, as if somehow content with what she had done, before picking up utensils and proceeding to eat.

I decided to risk another question. We seemed to spend an inordinate amount of time rushing here and there, this hilltop town, then Florence for a half day (quite pointless), sundry visits to Churches and Museums. In addition to the regulation beach visit. We never seemed to have enough time at La Caccia to sit down and relax and just look and think about painting. I tried to present this in a fairly non-confrontational way. Perhaps I should have been more direct.

'Look Paul, our job is to show them a bit of Italy, bone

them up on a bit of technique, feed and water them, and send them home to get on with it.'

I was going to say that there was nothing like that in my letter nor the brochure. But then I wasn't really prepared to argue. I mean, could I really afford to criticize at this stage, or even in the last resort, threaten to drop out? The main ones to suffer would be the students. Mariella's sights were now trained on last week's students. There had been only one man and he was in his eighties. 'Quite a few lonely hearts there. Pathetic really. Have to make sure we have a few more presentable men. We could advertise it as a singles dating holiday I suppose.' She was silent for a few seconds while she considered that. I remembered that when she had first written to me, quite a reasonable letter, offering me the post of tutor for four weeks, that I had been attracted by the name, Mariella Pagano, and, as an unattached male, had vaguely looked forward to meeting her. Within thirty seconds of our first meeting, I knew I had been mistaken. She seemed to be attractive in quite the wrong way, and I found myself looking for opportunities to escape from her company and specifically the assault course of chat and sarcastic comment. Fortunately during the day she was occupied with 'organising' the place and driving the minibus. The Italian she spoke was clearly a very recent acquisition. 'You can call me Mariella,' she said. Her real name, she told me when the students were out of hearing, was Mary Page but she thought the Italian would look better in the brochure.

The Japanese girl was onto another course. This one received the same treatment: inspection, adjustment, photograph, notebook, all done with a kind of reflection and poise verging on the reverent, but without being finicky or obsessive. Normally

I would have found her almost devotional manner disturbing. But there was something disarmingly tender and appreciative about the whole thing that dismissed my prejudices. Was she perhaps a food journalist, a travel writer, or an art photographer? None of it stopped her relishing the food or smiling shyly and graciously at the waiter.

Our own meal was coming to its conclusion. Mariella was 'up for coffee' as she said. It occurred to me I hadn't been asked anything about my own work as an artist. Of course it was not what we were about. It was the course and the members that counted. Nevertheless, in between the comments about the students, I had been supplied with plenty of information about Mariella's previous work in the City. 'A hot-house, Paul. They nurture you and then chop you down. Don't even think about it?' Then we were back to Italy. 'Next year plans are for Photography and Creative Writing. It's a gold mine. Holidays with a bit of culture and creativity. They're perceived as sexy. You can charge what you like.'

'Did you have someone in mind as a tutor? For the creative writing?'

'Hadn't thought about that angle yet. All else fails, I could give it a stab. Did I tell you I'm almost half way through a novel?'

The arrival of the coffee released me from the obligation to ask about that.

The Japanese girl had now finished her meal, having apparently decided against coffee. When her bill came, she discussed something with the waiter. He went off, and came back with a middle-aged woman in a pinafore and a youngish man. She asked them if she might photograph them, standing there by the table, and they duly obliged. All this of course eventually attracted the attention of Mariella.

'Sickening,' she said with a grunt. 'They photograph everything they can. Don't have time to look at anything, admire the beauty, atmosphere, cherish it, like you people, real artists. Just click and move on.'

I wanted to explain to Mariella what I had been observing, to correct her assumptions. But where would I start. And would she give me chance? The Japanese girl was now shaking the woman's hand, then her son's, then the waiter's. Her whole manner unobtrusive and polite, certainly not attention-seeking.

Then she left the restaurant. Mariella and I followed. We had already agreed to share the bill.

'I'll let you have my half when we get back to Catch,' she said.

As we walked back towards the station to pick up the next lucky party, I saw the Japanese girl sitting on a curved iron bench beneath a pendulous tree, apparently waiting for someone. For a second she caught my eye, and I think she smiled minutely. I wondered if she had heard any of what Mariella had been saying. And as we walked away from her, was she photographing us? And if so, what would she have written down about us in her notebook?

Lightning Source UK Ltd.
Milton Keynes UK

173389UK00001B/7/P

9 781848 767287